SAMMY FERAL'S
DIARIES OF

HELL HOUND
CURSE

Also by Eleanor Hawken

Sammy Feral's Diaries of Weird
Sammy Feral's Diaries of Weird: Yeti Rescue

SAMMY FERAL'S DIARIES OF

WEiRD

HELL HOUND CURSE

Eleanor Hawken

Illustrations by John Kelly

Quercus

New York • London

Quercus

New York • London

Text © 2013 by Eleanor Hawken
Illustrations © 2013 by John Kelly

First published in the United States by Quercus in 2014

ISBN 978-1-62365-813-7

Library of Congress Control Number: 2014931814

Distributed in the United States and Canada by
Hachette Book Group
237 Park Avenue
New York, NY 10017

Manufactured in the United States

2 4 6 8 10 9 7 5 3 1

www.quercus.com

For George and Oliver, two little legends

Saturday, September 5

Pay up or pack up!

That was the message Dad gave Donny and Red today.

Yes, they've been living at Feral Zoo rent-free for months. Yes, their pet collection of a gut worm, a phoenix, and a wish frog isn't exactly cute and cuddly. Yes, they look like weirdos of the highest degree and most normal people would rather swim with crocodiles than talk to them. Yes, they register a firm 7 on the Feral Scale of Weirdness. And they're my friends. In the last few months we've been through some tricky times together. They've helped me cure my werewolf family AND rescue a kidnapped yeti chief. Life without Donny and Red would be like a toothless great white shark . . . pointless. I can't believe Dad's asked them to leave!

DONNY
* **Job:** World-famous cryptozoologist (studies animals that supposedly don't exist).
* **Looks like:** Cool, calm alley cat with gray hair.
* **Talent:** He's a walking, talking crypto-encyclopedia.

RED
* **Job:** Donny's sidekick.
* **Looks like:** A gothic raccoon.
* **Talent:** Powers of telekinesis (she can move things with her mind!)

ME
* **Job:** Part-time zookeeper and apprentice cryptozoologist.
* **Looks like:** A freckly tree frog.
* **Talent:** CSC (Cross-Species Communication)— I can speak the languages of strange animals. Weird, right?

"It's just not fair!" I complained, as Donny pulled books about cryptozoology from the bookshelves and packed them away. "It's not like we're going to use the Backstage zoo area for anything else. You might as well live here."

"Kid's got a point," Red grunted. "That's the most sense he's spoken in months." Red's a sourpuss, but she's cool. I'd normally blast an awesome comeback at her when she says something like that. But today I decided to let her off on account of my dad making her homeless.

"Mr. Feral's a businessman." Donny shrugged. "I can see where he's coming from."

"Which is where? Wacko-land?" Red rolled her eyes.

Basically, as Dad explained it to me, Feral Zoo is having financial problems at the moment.

Financial problems = the most boring problems of all.

4

Who cares about money? Is money really a good reason to turn the world upside down . . . er, no!

But adults, my dad being one of them, seem to think that money is a good excuse for ruining my day . . . These were the reasons Dad gave:

* the price of animal feed is going up
* the price of electricity, water, and other stuff the zoo needs is going up
* Donny and Red use too much animal feed
* Donny and Red use too much electricity
* Donny and Red have to go

"All Mr. Feral said is that we can't carry on living here rent-free," Red said, taking Donny's books out of their boxes and placing them back on the shelves, using nothing but her powers of telekinesis. "So why don't we just start paying rent?"

"You know why. The cryptozoology business has been very quiet lately," said Donny sadly. "It's been months since we pulled in money from a case."

"Gwarrrk!"

A great noise came from the phoenix sitting in the corner of the room. Only I didn't hear the sound *Gwarrrk!* I heard the word *hungry.*

Phoenixes are just one of the strange animals whose language I can understand.

"The phoenix is hungry," I informed Donny.

"He's due to burst into flames any day now," Donny sighed. "He always eats more toward the end of his life cycle—gives him extra fuel to burn."

"But we haven't exactly been promoting the crypto-business lately," Red said, bringing our attention back to the matter in hand. "Maybe if I posted some flyers, whipped up a viral ad

campaign . . . a Facebook page . . . we might get a few more clients."

"Maybe," Donny agreed.

Whoop whoop! A glimmer of hope in the darkness of doom!

"But the problem isn't just us," Donny said, pulling the same books back off the shelf and giving Red the sort of look a Mongolian death worm might use to kill someone. "Feral Zoo is leaking money like a rusty pipe. Mr. Feral needs more than just our rent money to keep the business afloat."

"But it would be a good start," I said hopefully. "Look, you guys think about pulling in some money with your cryptozoology investigations, and I'll talk to my dad about other things we might be able to do."

"Sammy . . ." Donny started to object.

"Meet back here tomorrow morning," I interrupted. "And make sure you have something to report back!"

I ran out the door faster than you can say, "Cryptozoology." Donny and Red leaving the zoo was NOT up for discussion . . . I had other ideas!

I sent out this text to every member of my family:

Emergency family meeting
@ 8 in living room

These are the responses I got:

 Grace: Expect me to cancel my d8 with Max? I dnt think so!

 Natty: That's my bath time

 Dad: I'm working l8

 Mum: U have homework to do, young man!

I texted everyone back saying that this was way more important than dates with boyfriends, personal hygiene, homework, or eating cold takeout in the zoo office. This was a matter of life and death—the zoo's life and death!

This isn't the first time I've had to save Feral Zoo from disaster. A few months ago a crazy professor discovered that my family were actually werewolves (they're semi-cured now) and tried to blackmail us into giving him the zoo. Thankfully I was able to convince the world that the professor was as crazy as a sea otter on a surfboard and he's now locked up in a loony bin.

At 8 p.m. sharp Mom, Dad, Grace, Natty, myself, and Caliban (our ex-werewolf dog) gathered in the living room.

"You'd better make this quick, Sammy," my older sister, Grace, grumbled. Grace is moody at the best of times, but tomorrow is a full moon, and my ex-werewolf family gets seriously grouchy around this time of the month.

"Chill, sis," I said. "This is way more important than waxing your werewolf ear hair before a hot date."

Grace punched me on the arm and Caliban gave a playful yap of approval. Caliban loves a good fight.

"If this is about Donny and Red, Sammy, then I'll tell you what I told them," Dad said, looking even more tired than usual. "They can stay in the zoo if they can pay their way. If they can't, then they have to go—that's not unreasonable."

"Can we have their fire bird if they go?" Natty said.

"It's called a phoenix, Natty," I replied. "And, no—we can't. Not if you're going to look after it . . . We all know how you treat your pets."

"I didn't mean to kill Harry the hamster!"

she shrieked in protest. "I was just really, really hungry!"

"Sammy—hurry up and get to the point!" Mom said impatiently. "It's the full moon tomorrow, so we're all tired and grouchy."

"The point is, Mom," I said, shouting slightly more than I meant to, "that the zoo is in danger of closing down. And all because of money—no good reason at all if you ask me."

"How do you expect us to run a zoo with no money coming in?" Dad asked. "I don't want to raise the entry price. I love animals as much as you do, Sammy . . ."

Doubtful, I thought. When was the last time Dad cleaned out the spider tanks? *That's* love!

". . . But we're not running a charity," he continued. "Zoo animals need feeding. Zookeepers need paying. And we need money to do that."

"So let's raise the money," I said simply. "How hard can it be?"

"We could do camel rides for the kids!" Natty suggested.

Yes! Thank you, Natty! Why is my little sister the only one in my family with any bright ideas?

"And we could charge money for photos of zoo visitors with the birds of prey," Grace muttered. It was a good idea, but I got the impression Grace just wanted to get the meeting over and done with—her heart wasn't really in it.

"I suppose we could ask people to pay to adopt an animal," Dad said.

Now we're talking! "All excellent ideas!" I pitched in. "But we need to think even bigger . . ."

Mom scrunched her eyebrows together. "How about a fundraising soirée?"

I had no idea what "soirée" meant. It sounded like one of those fancy words adults use when they actually mean something really quite simple.

"What's a soirée?" Natty asked, so I didn't have to.

"A party," Grace replied.

See, "soirée" is totally a fancy word with a simple meaning. Hate words like that. Pointless-supreme!

"The tickets will cost £100 each and we'll hold an auction to help raise even more money," Mom suggested. "People can bid to feed the elephants or have a nighttime tour of the zoo."

"Great!" Dad said enthusiastically. "We could invite famous zoologists and celebrities," he went on. "We could ask them to donate something to be auctioned off. Maybe the local football team could give us a signed shirt."

"We could ask the Biker Boys to come!" Grace said excitedly. "Maybe they could donate their stage outfits for the auction!"

Natty squealed.

Mom nodded in approval.

Dad looked around for an explanation.

I groaned a groan of death. The Biker Boys? Really? The most pathetic, embarrassing, and cheesy boy band to ever record a musical note in the history of musical notes.

But fine—if it saved the zoo and stopped Donny and Red being kicked out, then I'd even put up with the Biker Boys. Talk about desperation!

"Then it's decided," Dad announced. "Let the zoo fundraising begin. Although it would still help if Donny and Red could start paying rent. In the meantime, we'll start planning the soirée tomorrow."

Grace deafened me with a squeal of delight.

"Party," I corrected Dad, clamping my hands over my ears.

Sunday, September 6

I went to the zoo straight after breakfast this morning. I had chores to do, but I figured cleaning out the sea lions could wait for an hour or two. First things first . . . I had to talk to Donny!

"Please give me some good news," I pleaded as I entered the Backstage yard. Donny was busy feeding his pet gut worm—a mega-dangerous three-headed snake that likes to eat people's guts. "I really need some good news."

"Hello, Sammy," came a small croak of a voice from the corner of the room.

"Wish Frog!" I smiled. "Have you heard about what's happening?"

He closed his bulging eyes and nodded his head slowly. It always amazes me that something so small can look so wise. "Yes, and I'll help in any way that I can. Although, be careful what you wish for . . ."

WISH FROG

* **Job**: Retired wish granter.
* **Looks like**: An Amazon horned frog.
* **Talent**: Has the AMAZING ability to grant wishes and speak dozens of languages, including English.
* **Freaky fact**: Everyone thought that wish frogs were extinct, but the last one was hiding at Feral Zoo!

Since he retired, the wish frog had sworn never to grant another wish again. But he has one left to fulfill. He granted me one after I saved his friend Bert the Yeti Chief from a crazy kidnapper. I'm saving it for an emergency—but I might have to use it soon if none of our fundraising ideas works.

"No luck with your family, Sammy?" Donny asked, as he threw a frozen field mouse into the gut worm's tank.

"Oh, they had plenty of bright ideas," I said miserably. "Including a fundraising party here in the zoo with the Biker Boys providing the soundtrack."

Red groaned like a creaking door. I knew I could count on a goth like her to hate boy bands as much as I do.

"Well, we do have some good news to report," Donny smiled, leaving the gut worm to munch its way through breakfast. Red and I followed him into the office.

Red summoned an old laptop with the power of her mind. "Check this out." She pointed to the screen. "I've set up a cryptozoology Facebook page."

She had as well.

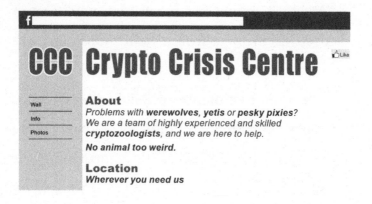

"We've had over 3,000 Likes already."

Result!

"Any good case leads?" I asked. I felt something land on my shoulder and looked down to see the wish frog sitting there peering at the screen.

20

"Mostly the usual false alarms," Donny said. "A yeti sighting . . ."

"We all know the yetis have left the country," Red said.

I scrolled through the list of inquiries. "UFOs . . ."

"Not our problem," Red mumbled.

"Unicorns."

"Ugh, as if we'd get involved with them!" she spat in disgust.

"Trolls," I read.

Donny scratched his head. "Now that could be interesting . . ."

"A Loch Ness monster sighting," I said. "That sounds good!"

Red rolled her eyes, "Anyone worth their crypto-salt knows Nessie was liberated from that dumpy lake years ago. He's swimming free in the North Atlantic now."

"And then there was this . . ." Donny said.

He pointed to a Facebook message . . .

 Dear Crypto Crisis Center,

I am on the run from certain death. You are my last hope.

About three weeks ago I was staying with my mother in the village of Devilbottom when her neighbor Old Mabel came back from her evening walk looking as pale as a sheet. She said she'd seen a ghostly dog in the graveyard. The very next morning she had died. Cause of death: spontaneous human combustion.

After Old Mabel's funeral I returned home to the town of Wraith. The next evening I bumped into my old friend Jimmy walking down the street. Jimmy was as white as snow—told me he'd seen a terrible, terrible thing—a ghostly black dog. Two days later Jimmy was pecked to death by a freak flock of angry pigeons.

Not wanting to meet the same ghastly fate as Jimmy, I fled Wraith. I traveled south and stayed with a friend in Shadowston. But the very next day I heard a shopkeeper telling a customer about a ghostly dog that had appeared to him the night before. That same day the shopkeeper died—slipped into a puddle and drowned.

Everywhere I go I hear the same story. A ghostly dog appears from nowhere, and if anyone sees him, their days are numbered.

I am now taking refuge in the small town of Banshee. My friend has kindly lent me her house while she is away on vacation. There have been no sightings of the dog here so far, but I know it's only a matter of time before it strikes again. I'm afraid that it's following me. Am I cursed?

I am a wealthy woman and I promise to reward you with £1 million if you can banish the beast for good.

Help.
Please.

Miss E. Oxley

"Wow! That's a lot of money," I said. "Enough for you to pay a lifetime of zoo rent. But a ghost dog? I've seen some crazy stuff this year . . . but surely there's no such thing?"

"It's not just a ghost dog," Donny said with a dangerous glint in his eye.

I know that look. It's the look he gets when he's on to something . . . an adventure.

"She's talking about the Hell Hound."

"The Hell Hound?" A cold shiver ran down my spine. "What's the—"

"SAMMY!" Mom's voice came from out in the yard. "You know you're not allowed back here until the sea lions are clean, and what have you done? Skipped out on your zoo chores! Again!"

"Coming, Mom," I groaned. The wish frog leaped from my shoulder as I turned to go. "Message her back," I told Donny.

"One step ahead of you," he grinned. "She's coming to the zoo tomorrow for a meeting."

"But if she's being haunted by the ghost of a dangerous dog, is it really a good idea for her to come—"

"SAMMY!" Mom screamed again.

"Gotta go," I muttered, running out of the

24

office. I should know by now not to tick Mom off at full-moon time—a recipe for disaster!

I did as I was told and cleaned out the sea lions. I also swept out the Galapagos penguins, the flightless cormorants, and the pelicans for good measure.

But all day long I had just one thought on my mind . . . the Hell Hound.

If it really exists then I'd rate it a healthy eight on the Feral Scale of Weirdness. But why would it be following Miss Oxley?

Can we really banish it for good?

Is this the only way we can save the zoo from financial ruin once and for all?

10 P.M.

It's past my bedtime, but Mom's got better things to do than give me a blasting for staying up late. So far this evening she's had to tell Natty off for howling at the moon too loudly, help Grace with a nose-hair-sprouting emergency, and fix Dad a raw beef burger. While Mom's been trying to keep my freaky family under control, I've been busy researching the Hell Hound on the Internet. Here's what I have so far:

HELL HOUND

* **Looks like:** A ghostly dog with eyes as red as glowing coals.
* **Natural habitat:** Walks between the land of the living and the land of the dead.
* **Last seen:** Shadowston (and Wraith and Devilbottom before that).
* **Deadly quality:** Inflicts a deadly curse upon anyone who looks it in the eye.
* **History:** The Hell Hound has featured in folklore all over the world for centuries.

The legend of the Hell Hound is obviously a famous one. One thing I've learned since meeting Donny and Red is that legends—especially ones about animals—are pretty much always true. Werewolves, yetis, Mongolian death worms—all true. There's no smoke without fire, and no animal too weird . . .

Monday, September 7

Today = 1st day back at school after the summer holidays.

The first day back at school is one of the most confusing days of the year. You see, today I'm happy because I finally get to see all my friends again after weeks away from them, but I'm also mega-bummed because I have to put on a school uniform and learn about boring things in a stuffy classroom. Confusing. I don't like confusing, I like simple. Black and white.

"Hey, Sammy!" my best friend Mark beamed at me when I met him at the school gates. Mark's got messy hair like a terrier's and the smile of a

cheeky chimp.
He tells the worst
jokes in the world,
and he knows
NOTHING
about my
freaky family,
or Donny and
Red, or my
strange ability
to speak to
weird animals.
It's often hard
to keep it that way.
"How was your
summer?"
he asked.

No way could I tell him about the Hell Hound,
so I thought back to the start of the summer
when I visited my grandparents on the Galapagos

Islands—on the other side of the world. "Yeah, it was cool. I saw marine iguanas and giant tortoises. How was yours?" I asked.

"We went to Disneyland and I threw up on the Space Mountain ride," he grinned. I knew that grin—it meant a joke was coming. "Hey, Sammy, how do spacemen pass the time on long trips?"

I raised my eyebrows in anticipation.

"They play astronauts and crosses!"

I groaned. It's good to know that Mark never changes.

The only interesting thing about my day at school was that Mrs. Palmer is making us write a project about something that we love for English class. We have to research it, write it, and then present it to the class.

I'm going to write mine on dangerous animals. I'm actually kind of psyched about it. I have tons of experience and know loads of cool facts about all sorts of dangerous animals, and I can't wait to share them with everyone.

I was so excited about my project, I forgot about the dreaded Hell Hound until lunchtime. As soon as I remembered I spent the whole afternoon fidgeting in class as if I had underpants full of fire ants. Miss Oxley was coming to the zoo today, and I couldn't wait to get out of school and hear what she had to say.

"Is she here?" I had run to Donny's office Backstage as soon as I got to the zoo. "Has she left already? What did she say? Do we know why the Hell Hound is haunting her? How can we stop it?"

"Whoa," Red raised her palms. "Negative, kid."

"What do you mean?" I asked quickly.

"Show him the message." Donny nodded in the direction of the computer.

Red floated the laptop through the air and it hovered before me.

Dear Crypto Crisis Center,

I'm sorry but I just don't feel safe enough to travel. I haven't left the house since I arrived in Banshee. I'm too afraid to step outside in case I see it. I want your help, I really do, but you're going to have to come to me.
I look forward to hearing from you.

Miss E. Oxley

My heart sank with disappointment. "She can't want our help that badly if she can't even be bothered to come to the zoo," I said gruffly.

"She's terrified for her life," Donny pointed out.

"So what now? Will we go and see her?" I asked.

"Yes, we'll make the trip. Banshee's not far," Donny said. "But we'll wait until this weekend. We need to spend a couple of days researching the Hell Hound—we need to know exactly what we're dealing with. Something tells me there's more to this case than meets the eye . . ."

Yes! Waiting until the weekend meant that I could go too.

"There's something else you need to see," Donny said seriously, pointing at the screen.

There was another message on the Crypto Crisis Facebook page.

I live in the small village of Devilbottom. This might sound crazy, but last night I saw a strange creature underneath the railway bridge. He was covered in warts and bent over a small fire cooking his dinner. I'm not sure what this creature was, but it didn't look human.

Mr. S. T. Range

"What kind of creature is covered in warts and lives under a bridge?" I asked.

"A troll," Donny and Red said at the same time.

"And the village of Devilbottom," I said. "Why does that sound familiar?"

"Because that's where the Hell Hound appeared first, according to Miss Oxley," Donny said.

"A troll and the Hell Hound in the same village? Is that a coincidence?" I asked.

"Maybe," Donny admitted. "But we can't ignore the possibility that the sightings are linked."

"So now we have a troll *and* the Hell Hound to worry about! What do we do?" I asked.

"The three Rs." Donny grinned. "Research. Research. Research."

"That's one R repeated," I pointed out.

"It's so important we say it three times," Red muttered.

So I guess that's what the next few days will be about: research, research, research. On the Internet, in books, in the local papers. With so much to do, I wonder when I'm going to have time to write my dangerous-animals project for school.

When I first asked Donny to train me as a cryptozoologist, I hadn't really thought it through. How am I ever going to juggle school with saving the world from weird animals? Maybe Mom and Dad will understand and let me drop out of school? Unlikely.

One thing that I do know is that Donny is right—we cannot go anywhere near the Hell Hound unless we're completely prepared. Otherwise we might as well look the creature right in the eye. And then, just like the dinosaurs and dodos, we'll be history . . .

Tuesday, September 8

Mark came to hang out at the zoo after school today. Yes, I needed to do research into the Hell Hound, but I hadn't seen Mark all summer. As much as I like Donny and Red, it is good to have a normal friend too. Even if he does tell the worst jokes in the world.

I'm going to be hearing a lot of Mark's bad jokes over the next few days. As we walked through the zoo, Mark's phone beeped. He read a text message and turned to me with a huge grin.

"Guess what! Mom says I can come stay with you this weekend," Mark said excitedly. "I didn't want to say anything earlier, in case she changed her mind."

Excuse me?

"Mom and Dad are going to a medical conference for a few days," he explained as I looked at him blankly. "Your parents said I could stay with you while they're away."

Hmm, not the best timing in the world considering I'm meant to be investigating the Hell Hound this weekend . . . How would I keep it a secret? "Why don't you stay with your Aunt Mildred?" I asked.

Mark looked a bit hurt. "I'd much rather stay with you, Sammy. Aunt Mildred has more facial hair than a bearded pig. And she gives the world's sloppiest kisses."

Mark's right. No one should have to suffer sloppy kisses from a half-woman, half–bearded pig.

"No, of course," I said, trying to backtrack and sound like a best friend should. "It'll be awesome. We can spend the weekend working at the zoo—you'll make a good zookeeper. We could get some practice in now if you want. What do you wanna do first? Feed the snakes? Pick out bones from the vulture den? Ooh, I know—we have a load of crocodile eggs that are about to hatch. We could—"

"What about your other friends that live here?" Mark asked. "The guy with gray hair and the girl with red hair."

Hmm, that was one thing I did NOT want to talk about. There was no way I could introduce him to Donny and Red—I couldn't let him see their pets and get a glimpse into their crazy world. My crazy world.

"I know you hang out with them whenever you're here," he added quietly. "If I'm gonna be staying with you and helping out at the zoo, then you might as well tell me. Are they zookeepers too?"

"Yes," I said quickly. "Kind of. It's their day off though."

Mark's eyes narrowed in suspicion. I hated lying, but I'd done a lot of lying to Mark since my life boarded the weirdo train.

"Fine," he sulked. "Have it your way. Let's just hang out in the reptile house and we can talk about our school projects. I'm going to write mine on roller coasters. Did you know that the first roller coaster was built over 200 years ago in Russia by Catherine the Great?"

I did not. That's one of the great things about Mark. He's super-clever and knows loads of cool facts about random things.

So after swinging by the zoo café to pick up snacks (I had potato chips and a peanut-butter sandwich and Mark had fruit—boring) we hung out in the reptile house. I fed my pet python, Beelzebub, Mark collected some snake skins from the anaconda tanks (they work really well in an anti-werewolf potion by the way), and we talked about our projects. I told him facts about the world's deadliest animals. "Did you know there's a water snail so poisonous that its sting will kill you in five minutes flat? It's called the cone snail."

And he told me more cool things about roller coasters. "The world's highest roller coaster is in America and it's over 139 meters tall!"

It felt good to hang out and talk about normal stuff. Man, I hadn't realized how much I'd missed Mark.

As I was putting Beelzebub back in his tank I saw a bright red head of hair poke around the reptile-house door.

"I thought you said she had a day off," Mark said suspiciously.

Oh, whoopee-whoopee-doo-dah! Trust Red to ruin a brief moment of normality.

"I must have misread the zoo staff schedule," I mumbled.

"Sammy!" Red shouted. "Can I have a word?"

Red never wants to speak to me, so this could only mean one thing—the Feral Scale of Weirdness was about to skyrocket.

I sighed and looked apologetically at Mark. "I'll be back in a minute."

Feeling guilty, I quickly slipped out of the reptile house to find Red *and* Donny standing outside.

Both of them? Uh-oh, this was bad news.

"I thought you were meant to be researching the Hell Hound?" Red said, crossing her arms and glaring at me. "We're relying on you, Sammy. There's so much to do. We're going to Banshee this weekend to investigate the Hell Hound. We would have done some research ourselves, but we've had another troll sighting reported . . ."

"Chill out." I rolled my eyes. "Firstly, I'll get on Google later and do some research. Excuse me for having a life. And secondly, what do you mean, 'troll sighting'?"

"Another person has reported a strange creature underneath a railway bridge," Donny said quickly. "It's dangerous to ignore it—I'll need to go and investigate."

"Can I come?" I asked hopefully.

"No, Sammy." Red glared at me. "We need you here, doing more Hell Hound research. If we're going to Banshee this weekend, then we need to be prepared."

Troll hunting = cool.

Research = boring.

My life = unfair!

"But you need me there," I said, annoyed. "I don't want to wait until we go to Banshee for the weekend, I want to come with you now. I'm the only one who can speak the troll's language. If you go without me, it'll be dangerous."

Red gave me a devilish smile. "Cryptozoology's dangerous, kid. But that's the way we roll . . ."

"What's cryptozoology?" came a voice from behind me. "And where's Banshee?"

Mark.

Freak-out time!

The word "cryptozoology" sounded so, so wrong coming out of Mark's mouth. This was Mark, the most normal thing in my life—I didn't want him to know that word. I didn't want my two worlds to collide.

My brain went into uber-panic mode . . . How long had he been standing there? How much had he heard? Exactly how much explaining did I have to do?

"Sammy . . ." Mark tugged on my arm, snapping me out of my panic trance. "What's cryptozoology?" he repeated.

Words tumbled out of my mouth before I could stop them, "Cryptozoology is the study of animals that don't exist. Like yetis, or dragons, or werewolves."

Red raised her eyebrows at me—I silently begged her not to tell Mark the truth. That werewolves, and all the other weird animals out there, actually did exist: they were as real as a cone snail's sting.

Mark looked mega-confused. "Why are you talking about that?" he asked Donny.

Donny started to explain, "Because I'm a cryptozoo—"

"That's enough!" I panicked, dragging Mark back into the reptile house, away from Donny and Red.

"Why don't you want me to talk to your friends?" Mark said angrily. "Aren't I cool enough? Isn't my hair weird enough?"

"That's not it," I said, feeling flustered.

How could I begin to explain the truth to Mark

now? I just did not want him to know. I had to keep Mark and everything normal as far down the Feral Scale of Weirdness as was humanly possible.

"Well, if I *am* cool enough to hang out with you guys then I guess I can come along on your trip to Banshee this weekend."

ALARM BELLS!

No. Way.

"That's not a good idea, Mark," I said, trying to stay calm.

"Er, in case you'd forgotten, Sammy, I'm supposed to be staying with you," he pointed out. "You can't just dump me for the weird-hair brigade and leave me to play Happy Hamster Families with Natty."

That's when it struck me. Mark was right. I couldn't go off to Banshee leaving him with my family. He didn't know the truth about them either—that they're all secretly ex-werewolves. There was no way he could survive a few days in the Feral house without finding out what a freak patrol my family actually is. What was my mom thinking by inviting him to stay? Maybe it would be better if he comes with us to Banshee—at least that way I could follow him around like a shadow, just to make sure our secrets stay hidden. My mind was buzzing—what a nightmare!

I can't believe what I said next. "Fine."

Mark grinned like a demented chipmunk who's just landed a prize-winning nut. I have to admit, it felt good to see him look that happy.

"Cool!" He beamed.

So that's decided then. Mark will be the little slice of normal in our wacky weirdo pie this Saturday.

Now I just have to try to figure out how to hide all the crypto-craziness from him . . .

Wednesday, September 9

Only three days to go before I get dangerously close to the Hell Hound. Only two days before Mark comes to stay with me and has his official introduction to my weird world. There's no time to waste. I have to prepare myself for whatever's going to happen this weekend, and I need to be as clued-in as possible on the Hell Hound.

Donny and Red had obviously been doing their crypto-homework, and I wasn't about to be left behind. If I want to be a real-life cryptozoologist, like Donny, then I need to take my training seriously.

After school I swung by the library to look at books on mythical animals. Sure, Donny has a mountain of books Backstage, but most of them are in languages I can't understand. I found three interesting ones in the library: *Magical Lands and Mythical Animals, Beasts of Folklore,* and *Creatures of Doom.*

I've spent the evening reading the sections on the Hell Hound (and also the sections on werewolves, seeing as my family are all ex-wolves—didn't learn anything new though). I now know enough to write my own Hell Hound guide . . .

Sammy Feral's Guide to the Hell Hound

Chapter 1:
An Introduction

* It sometimes appears headless or floating on a carpet of mist.

* It likes to haunt graveyards, cross-roads, and dark forests.

* It's often reported to smell terrible and can be smelled before it's seen—a good warning sign to **RUN!**

One thing I didn't find out is any link the Hell Hound might have with trolls. Maybe Donny's wrong, and it is just a coincidence that the Hell Hound and a troll were spotted in the same village.

I was reading in bed when my phone buzzed with a text. It was from Donny:

Y didn't U come 2 the zoo 2nite?

I texted him back:

Busy researching. See U 2morrow

Donny texted back right away:

I'll B out investigating troll sightings. Red will B here

Great. Dealing with Red on her own is like swimming in a tank of cone snails with my eyes closed. I wish I could go troll hunting with Donny instead!

Thursday, September 10

Say anything you want about my crazy family, but when they say they're going to do something, they do it in style!

Fundraising at the zoo started today. Now you can pay to have your picture taken with Humphrey the hawk, or sponsor an animal of your choice. So far the monkeys and chimps have been snapped up like a piranha feeding frenzy!

I wish I could have been there the whole day to help out, but obviously I had to be in school. Don't people understand that I could be more use if I didn't have to spend so much of my time in a classroom?

"Absolutely not," Dad said when I asked him if I could drop out of school.

Predictable or what?

"You're only twelve years old and you need to finish your education." We were standing watching people have their picture taken with Humphrey (the only hawk at Feral Zoo who won't peck your nose off and fly away with it). The line was gigantic— we must have made a fortune today from hawk pictures alone.

"But, Dad," I protested, "think of all the things I could help out with here at the zoo if I didn't go to school. I could help with more feeding, and cleaning, and fundraising." I leaned in and said the next bit quietly so no one else could hear. "Not to mention all the things I could help out with Backstage."

"The answer's no, Sammy," Dad said again.

Not. Fair!

Normally Dad's good at giving in to me, but I could see that he was not going to budge on this one.

I spent the rest of the evening helping zoo visitors have their picture taken with Humphrey. Humphrey did really well—he didn't peck any eyes out and he didn't even poop on anyone. Result!

After I'd put Humphrey back into his enclosure, I had just enough time to pop Backstage to see Red.

"I was just learning to tolerate you, kid," Red said, as soon as she saw me. She was feeding Donny's fire-breathing turtle—levitating food

into its cage and then
ducking out of the
way as it burped
flames at her.

"But inviting
your little
friend along
on Saturday is a
bad idea. I have to
deal with two of you
numbskulls now."

"I'm not a numbskull," I said, annoyed. "And neither is Mark. Just give him a chance."

"Sure." She shrugged. "So long as he knows what he's getting himself into."

I gulped.

Of course Mark doesn't have the faintest inkling what he's getting himself into. I haven't told him the truth. Could he even handle the truth?

"Obviously we've always preferred to work alone," Red said with a miserable scowl, dodging another fiery burp from the fire-breathing turtle. "But since you came along, we've realized that having an extra pair of hands isn't a bad thing. And your talent certainly comes in handy."

She was talking about my CSC—Cross-Species Communication—my ability to understand the languages of strange animals.

"So Donny's out hunting for trolls, huh?" I asked. "You really think there's a link between the Hell Hound and a troll?"

"Even if there isn't a link, a troll report isn't something we can ignore. Trolls can be dangerous."

"How?"

Red shrugged. "Oh, you know, child-snatching, bone-munching. The usual," she said casually.

Um, I do not like the sound of that!

"So far this troll's not hurt anyone," Red said, sounding almost disappointed. "But Donny's gone to check it out anyway."

Too right! There's no way I want to be snatched and munched by a troll.

"How's the Hell Hound Internet research coming along?" Red asked.

"Umm," I murmured. Red shook her head impatiently. "It's tough trying to find time for crypto-research around schoolwork and zoo chores," I said defensively.

"Well, make time," she snapped. "We're going to Banshee this weekend—and research could be the difference between life and death."

I spent hours this evening trying to do more Hell Hound research online. But there's no new info since the last time I looked. I guess no one's seen the Hell Hound and lived to tell the tale—otherwise there'd be more written about it.

Disheartened, I gave up on the Hell Hound and spent the rest of the evening researching dangerous animals instead. I left out werewolves, trolls, and Mongolian death worms and kept it strictly to run-of-the-mill animals that can kill.

Working on the project was a good distraction from thinking about Saturday, when Mark joins us on our crypto–field trip.

The Hell Hound sounds like bad news. And I don't want Mark to find out about it, or the troll, or any other strange crypto-creature that might appear on the scene. Letting him get too close to crypto-business is a terrible idea. But I can't get out of it now . . . can I?

Friday, September 11

Today I gave my presentation about dangerous animals to the class.

They. Love. Me.

Result!

Maybe I shouldn't be a cryptozoologist when I grow up. Maybe I should be a teacher or someone who gives interesting talks to people.

Oh, who am I kidding . . . ? Being a cryptozoologist is way cooler!

I had some time at the end of my talk so the other kids in my class got to ask me questions:

Tommy:	What's the most dangerous animal known to man?
Me:	A mosquito. Mosquito bites are responsible for over 3 million deaths per year.
Katarina:	What's your favorite dangerous animal?
Me:	Ummm, probably a blue-ringed octopus—it's only as big as a golf ball but holds enough venom to kill 26 adults, and there's no known cure.
Mark:	Who held the octopus for ransom?
Me:	*Groan.*
Mark:	Squidnappers!

After school Mark came home with me. That's it now—he's here. No getting rid of him, no matter what might lie in store. Donny and Red are picking us up first thing in the morning to go to Banshee and speak to Miss Oxley. I've learned next to nothing from all the research I've done—who knows what we'll be faced with there. I feel mega-anxious—there are just so many things that could go wrong.

And honestly, just getting Mark through this evening was an achievement. He's known my family since we were little kids, so he's pretty used to their weird ways. He didn't bat an eyelid when Grace stomped all over the house complaining that she STILL hadn't heard back from the Biker Boys about the zoo party—Mark's seen Grace in a snit a hundred times before. However, explaining Natty's behavior was more of a challenge . . .

"Do you want to see the picture I drew in school today, Mark?" she asked with a big toothy grin.

"Sure, Natty." Mark smiled. He's always been way more patient with her than I have. I guess it's because he doesn't actually have to *live* with the half-girl, half–squirrel monkey.

My heart nearly leaped out of my chest and splatted all over Natty's picture when she held it up for Mark to see. It was a picture of a werewolf tearing a small animal to shreds (I think it was a guinea pig but I'm not sure—Natty's not a great artist). A firm 5 on the Feral Scale of Weirdness, for sure.

Mark gulped and threw me a worried look. "It's, um . . . very lifelike," was all he could say.

"I wanted to do more blood," Natty said matter-of-factly, "but the teacher wouldn't let me."

Thankfully that was the only tricky event of the evening. The rest of the time my family did a good job of acting normal. Mom even went to the effort of making normal food for dinner: roast chicken and french fries. Yum.

"So, how long have you known Donny and Red?" Mark asked me as we were brushing our teeth.

"Um," I spat my toothpaste out. "A few months. They help out at the zoo a lot." That wasn't a lie . . . but I didn't mention that the things they help out with are not exactly regular zookeeping duties. Ever seen Red sweep out the skunk enclosure? Er, no.

"They don't seem like normal zookeepers to me," Mark said.

Maybe at that point I should have just been honest. I should have just told Mark the truth about Donny and Red and what they do.

"They're part-time storm chasers," I lied. "That's why we're going to Banshee. Freak weather patterns."

Er, attack of the numbskull nitwit!

Storm chasers? Freak weather patterns? Seriously? What was I thinking?

Mark nodded. "I guess that makes sense. That must be why Donny has such gray hair—the wind has blown all the color away!"

Phew—my lie had worked! I'd put Mark off the scent. But it wouldn't be for long . . .

Mark is sleeping on a cot in my bedroom. At the moment he's reading a book about wasps while I write in my diary. He keeps interrupting me to tell me wasp facts. "Did you know that a male wasp is called a drone, and it's only the female wasps that sting?"

"Cool," I said. I love learning animal facts. "Where did you get the book from?"

"Mom and Dad gave it to me," Mark said. "So if I see a wasp I'll know what to do."

Mark's parents are mega-worriers. They're both doctors and are both obsessed with Mark

catching some weird disease or dying in some horrible way. Apart from wasp-defense, Mark's parents have also made him bring everything but the kitchen sink. Honestly, I once spent the night in the zoo's reptile house with nothing but a roll of tin foil to keep me warm. But Mark has brought a sleeping bag, a roll mat, food, spare pajamas, clean socks (er, what's wrong with the ones he wore today?), and a list of emergency telephone numbers.

I'm tempted to call Mark's parents weird, but then again, my parents are werewolves . . . so I'll stay quiet on that one.

"Mark?" I said, as he put away his book and turned off his bedside lamp. "Are you nervous about tomorrow?"

He laughed. "What a strange question. Why would I be nervous?"

If only he knew.

I feel bad for not warning him.

Mark has no idea what he's getting himself into. He might know how to fend off an angry female wasp, but protect himself from the Hell Hound? He won't have a clue.

Maybe I'm not being a good friend by letting

him tag along tomorrow. Maybe I'm the worst friend in the history of friendships.

I guess we'll know either way after tomorrow . . .

Saturday, September 12

Today was far and away, without a shadow of a doubt, most definitely, utterly, 100 percent, THE WORST DAY OF MY LIFE!!!

This is what happened . . .

Mark and I arrived at the zoo this morning and clambered into Donny's van. Thankfully the wish frog had decided to stay in his tank—I wasn't looking forward to explaining my talking frog friend to Mark.

"Settle in. It's a two-hour drive," Donny informed us as he revved up the engine.

"I brought my book on wasps," Mark said proudly.

Red turned around from the front seat and gave Mark a look that made him shrink back into his chair in shame. "I think wasps are cool," I reassured him. "Ignore Red. I always do."

"I find that reading in the car really helps my car sickness," Mark muttered.

Er, brain-fart! Am I completely and utterly insane? Has my memory been wiped? Why didn't I remember that Mark has the worst car sickness known to man?

Mark = the Pukatron.

He's been puking in cars for as long as I've known him.

And the wasp book did not help. At all.

We'd only been on the road for five minutes when Mark said weakly, "Pull over . . . I think I'm going to be . . ."

And then he upchucked all over the back seat of Donny's van, all over his wasp book, and all over me.

This was reason number one for my day being *completely awful*!

Mark was sick four more times before we arrived at the village of Banshee. Donny found an old tennis shoe in the trunk and gave it to Mark to be sick in. Red spent the journey pinching her nose and muttering under her breath. I'm not going to write down what she was saying, because it was really rude.

I stupidly thought that the day couldn't get any worse. I was so, so wrong . . .

"I feel much better now," Mark said with a weak smile as we eventually pulled up in Banshee. "This seems, um . . ." Mark glanced around at the tiny village. He looked completely befuddled. "It doesn't look to me like the kind of place that has freak weather patterns though. It's not exactly tornado territory. Why are we here?"

Donny spoke before I could. "Don't you know? We're here to investigate—"

"Sandwiches," I interrupted quickly. "Yes, um, apparently this village has the best, er, sandwich shop in the country."

A huge smile erupted across Mark's chimp-like face. "Great! I love sandwiches! And I'm mega-hungry after throwing up my breakfast." Mark set off down the street, looking all around him.

Red rolled her eyes. "Well, you two can try to find the sandwich shop while Donny and I take care of some business."

"What? Wait—I want to come," I hissed.

"We're not going to see Miss Oxley right away," Donny whispered back. "I want to take a look about first. We need to ask around, make sure there haven't been any Hell Hound sightings since she's been here."

"Catch you kids later," Red muttered, before she and Donny walked off in the other direction.

"What are they up to?" Mark asked curiously as I joined him.

"They've gone to talk to a tornado enthusiast who lives here," I lied. "I thought we'd leave them to it and go find this sandwich shop."

Mark grinned. "Good plan."

We spent the next hour walking around the tiny village of Banshee. There wasn't much there—a duck pond, a small school, and an old church with a graveyard. I looked around for Hell Hound clues, but there was nothing to report. Eventually we found a sandwich shop. "This must be it," I said.

Mark flashed me a confused look. The sandwich shop did not look good. The windows were inch-thick with grime, the shop sign was half hanging off and the greasy man behind the counter was coughing and sneezing all over the bread rolls. I would rather have eaten my lunch off a blue-ringed octopus's backside than buy something from there.

"This place?" Mark looked at me skeptically.

I shrugged pathetically. "Looks can be deceiving."

Bravely we both ordered sandwiches from the shop of grossness. I had ham and mayo on a brown roll. Mark—greedier than a Hogzilla pig—ordered two: cheese and onion *and* tuna mayonnaise.

We took our sandwiches to the duck pond and ate them on a nearby bench. "Mmmm," Mark mumbled with his mouth full. "There's something . . ." He put a finger in his mouth and pulled out what looked like a toenail. "I think this was in my sandwich," he said, his face pale.

Mark's toenail toasty was reason number two that my day was dreadful.

"I'll save this tuna sandwich for the way back," Mark announced as we walked away from the duck pond.

In the distance I could see two heads—one gray, one red—walking toward us.

"Hey, Sammy. Hey, Mark." Donny pushed his gray hair out of his eyes. "Good thing we ran into you. We're just about to go and have a cup of tea with Miss Oxley. Coming?"

"I could use a cup of tea," said Mark, nodding. "Who's Miss Oxley? Another tornado enthusiast?"

Er, panic time! This was it, the moment I'd been dreading ever since Mark decided he was coming to Banshee with us. My best friend was about to come face to face with proof that the world is a weird, weird place. The proof? Miss Oxley. A woman on the run from a Hell Hound Curse.

"Miss Oxley's as batty as a fruit bat," I said. "Ignore everything she says. She's crazy."

Miss Oxley was staying in her friend's house, just as her message had said. The house was more like a mansion. It had stone pillars either side of the front door and a large front lawn. A sprinkler system sprang to life as we walked up the garden path, almost drenching us. The doorbell chimed like old church bells, and soon enough a very large lady in a purple dress opened the door.

"You must be Donny." She smiled sadly. "I'm Miss Oxley."

"These are my colleagues," Donny said as we followed Miss Oxley into the living room. We sat down on a plush golden couch and she began to pour us all tea from a china teapot.

"It would be cool if we really were all Donny's storm-chaser colleagues," Mark whispered to me. Red must have heard him as she narrowed her eyes in a confused squint.

"Thank you for coming here today. I'm sorry I couldn't come to you." Miss Oxley pulled a flowery handkerchief from her sleeve and dabbed at her glistening eyes. "But when you've seen so many people meet a terrible end . . ."

Mark took a loud slurp of his tea and asked, "Were they killed in a storm?"

Confusion passed over Miss Oxley's face, but before I could jump in with an answer she said, "No, dear. They were killed by the Hell Hound Curse."

I held my breath, not daring to look at Mark. This was it, it had finally happened—my friend was being given a glimpse into my wacky world.

"Please," Donny said quietly to Miss Oxley, not even looking at Mark, "we need to try to understand the link between the attacks."

"Attacks?" Mark blurted loudly.

Donny ignored him and carried on. "You described them in your message. But maybe you could tell us what happened in a bit more detail. We need to establish why the Hell Hound might be following you."

I took a deep breath and glanced at Mark. He looked as if he was about to burst out laughing. As he caught my eye I mouthed the word, "Crazy," and nodded toward Miss Oxley.

But the smile slowly fell from Mark's face as Miss Oxley told her story. We listened in silence as she told us all about the Hell Hound attacks in every last grisly detail. It was bad, *really, really* bad. The terrible smell, the ghostly dog with its eyes of flame, and the freak accidents that no one survived. "Everywhere I go, someone sees this dog and then they die. It's only a matter of time before it happens to someone here in Banshee. I just don't understand why it hasn't come for me. I mean, it must be me that it's after. Why else would it be following me from village to village?" she said.

"Since you contacted us we've researched every documented case of the Hell Hound," Donny said, scratching his head. "Every attack is the same, and they're just as you have described. No one has ever survived. But there's no record at all of the Hell Hound ever following someone. And after coming here today and meeting you, I think what we're dealing with here is a case of very bad luck. You were just in the wrong place at the wrong time, every time. Miss Oxley, I don't think the Hell Hound is after you—

it's just happened to appear in the same places as you."

Miss Oxley let out a big sigh. "Well, that's certainly good to hear. But if it's not me that's making it travel about like this, what is?"

"That's what we need to find out." Donny paused, then said, "I don't suppose you've heard rumors of any other strange creatures in the towns where the Hell Hound has appeared?"

Miss Oxley shook her head. "Like what?"

"Like a troll?" Donny asked.

"No, I've not heard anything like that. Why? Have people seen trolls too?" She shook her head in disbelief. "Whatever next? Leprechauns? Dragons? Unicorns?"

"If you're unlucky enough to see a unicorn, stay well away," Red said bluntly. "They bite."

"I don't think I'll ever leave the house again," Miss Oxley said, her eyes wide.

I glanced in Mark's direction. He was looking

81

at me as though I was a total stranger—as if he didn't know me at all.

Neither Mark nor I said a word as Donny and Red thanked Miss Oxley for the tea and she thanked us for coming. She showed us out of her house and we walked back up the garden path, the sprinklers still watering the huge lawn on either side of us.

It was getting dark outside, time for us to be getting back to Feral Zoo. We walked to the van in silence.

"What a load of crap!" Mark giggled nervously. "That lady was as crazy as a box of frogs on a Sunday. Batty. But she made a good cup of tea, and good cookies, and . . . Oh no, Sammy . . ."

"What?" I gulped, just waiting . . . waiting for him to ask me what was really going on.

"I left my tuna sandwich back at Miss Oxley's house. I'll just run back and get it—I'll meet you guys at the van."

82

I nodded with relief. Maybe I wouldn't have to tell Mark the whole truth. He hadn't put two and two together—he just thought Miss Oxley was crazy. I wouldn't have to tell him that the Hell Hound was real.

At least with Mark off on the hunt for his missing tuna sandwich I had a chance to catch up with Donny and Red. "Did you find out anything interesting when you were looking around the village this morning?"

"No." Red shook her head. "We asked around but no one has seen the Hell Hound, thank goodness."

"I think Miss Oxley is wise to stay here," Donny added. "Banshee seems like a safe place. There haven't been any sightings, and I can't see why the Hell Hound would want to come here. There's nothing but a duck pond, a bad sandwich shop, and an old graveyard."

"But what was so different about the other

places the Hell Hound appeared in?" I wondered aloud. "I mean, it's never appeared in the same place twice. And how does it choose its victims?"

Red fiddled with the skull necklace around her neck. She does that a lot when she's thinking. "You never know where it'll hit. But one thing's for certain—we need to stop the Hell Hound striking again."

We arrived back at the car and waited for Mark.

We waited.

And waited.

And waited.

Eventually Mark came running around the corner. I knew as soon as I saw him that something terrible had happened. I knew that I would remember this day for the rest of my life. The day that I wished I could live again, just so I could do everything differently.

Mark was as white as a sheet. His eyes were

wide with panic and fear, his hands shaking like a leaf.

"I saw it," was all he managed to say. "The Hell Hound. It's coming for me."

Sunday, September 13

Sammy Feral = executioner.

Well, I might as well be an executioner. I was the one who let Mark tag along to Banshee—putting him smack dab in the path of the Hell Hound. And if he hadn't seen the Hell Hound, he wouldn't have been sentenced to a terrible death.

I couldn't bring myself to write anything else in my diary last night. The only good thing that happened yesterday was that Mark was so shocked by the sight of the Hell Hound he didn't puke once on the way home. Who would have thought that seeing the Hell Hound could cure carsickness?

He spent the whole journey staring out of the window, not saying a word. Red even offered him chocolate and he just ignored her. I've never seen Red be that friendly to anyone before so I knew she was worried. The situation was desperate.

I even tried telling Mark a bad joke to snap him out of his daze. "Hey, Mark, why did the Hell Hound chase its own tail? Because no one else would!" Mark didn't even smile. He didn't even hear me. And honestly, I don't blame him. I'd be staring into space like a zombie too if I'd just come face-to-face with my own death.

We headed Backstage at the zoo as soon as we could and Donny sat Mark down on a chair. Red made him a cup of tea and forced it into his hand. Mark just stared at the floor, his eyes unblinking.

"Mark, buddy," I said softly, "we're going to help you. I promise. But first you need to tell us exactly what happened. It might not even have been the Hell Hound you saw; it might just have been a great big—"

"Its eyes . . ." Mark's voice was a pathetic croak. "The eyes of death."

"Tell us, Mark," Donny said. "Tell us everything you saw."

Mark lifted his gaze from the floor and stared straight at me. I felt my skin prickle with fear as he slowly began to speak . . .

"I picked up my tuna sandwich from Miss Oxley's house, and I was heading back to you. I cut through the graveyard. I wouldn't have if I'd thought the story was true. There's no such thing as ghosts . . . right . . . no such thing as a ghost dog . . . as the Hell Hound?" Mark's eyes were begging us to tell him it wasn't true.

I hung my head in shame. It was all true.

"As I walked through the graveyard I was staring at the ground thinking about all the wasps hibernating at this time of year." He took a deep breath and swallowed hard. He shut his eyes and told the rest of the story with them closed, as if he couldn't bring himself to look at anyone. "First came the smell—like rotten eggs and trash cans on a hot day. Then I saw its feet— ghostly dog paws which looked like smoke and shadows. Then I looked up and saw its huge body. A black shadow, a beast so terrifying I knew I wasn't imagining it . . . There is nothing in my imagination that looks like that. Its mouth hung open and I could see its terrible teeth. And its eyes . . . burning red . . . evil. As soon as I looked into them I knew my days were numbered.

Please don't tell my mom . . ." he said quietly. "She'll be so angry."

"We're going to find a way to save you, don't worry," Donny said firmly. "You must stay here for now, where we can keep you safe."

"Yes, it's a good thing your parents are away for a few more days," I said. "You're better off with us."

That's when I called my parents and made up an excuse to stay at the zoo last night. "Beelzebub is sick," I lied. "I'm going to stay at the zoo until he gets better. It might be a couple of days. Mark's here too—he's keeping me company."

"Okay, Sammy, but Monday's a school day," Mom reminded me over the phone.

Here we go again . . . School is getting in the way of EVERYTHING.

"So don't go to bed too late," Mom warned me.

"Won't. Promise. Thanks, Mom," I said quickly, putting the phone down before she could get suspicious.

So Mark and I spent last night sleeping Backstage at the zoo. Mark was still so traumatized he didn't even ask about Donny's pets. I'm going to have some major explaining to do once all this is over.

9 P.M.

We haven't left the Backstage offices all day. So far we've managed to keep Mark alive.

We have mostly spent the day death-proofing Backstage. We've done this by:

* a thorough electrical check
* removing all sharp objects
* wrapping every sharp furniture corner in cotton wool

Mark spent the whole day sitting on a chair next to the phoenix, staring at his wasp book but never turning the page. Every now and again he looked up at the phoenix and blinked in confusion—but he didn't once ask any questions. Even when the bird burst into flames and blasted phoenix fluff and ash all over him, he just sat there with a hat of colorful feathers—staring into space.

I tried to speak to him: "Hey, Mark, you hungry?"

Silence.

"Hey, Mark, want to help me clean out the phoenix ashes?"

Blink, blink. Silence.

"Mark, just talk to me. I'll answer any question you have . . ."

Silence. Silence. Silence.

It was as if he was in some kind of trance.

"He's in shock," Red told me as I stared at Mark worriedly.

I don't blame him for being in a state of shock. It's a lot to take in. The whole situation is so bad I can't even bring myself to rate it on the Feral Scale of Weirdness. I'm just pleased the wish frog hasn't hopped over to say hi today. No way is Mark in a fit state to meet him. The Hell Hound and a self-combusting phoenix are more than enough for now.

Mark might not be speaking, but at least he isn't dead. And so far we've seen no sign of danger.

Mark: 1; Hell Hound Curse: 0.

We're spending another night at the zoo. It's safer here. But I know the Hound will come for him. And when it does, I need to be ready.

Monday, September 14

I awoke to the sound of screaming.

Blood-curdling screams.

Mark screaming for his life.

"Get it off me!" he wailed in pure panic.

Donny's gut worm had somehow broken out of its cage and was attacking Mark. The creature reared up, hissing into the air, ready to strike. All three heads tilted back and bared their razor-sharp fangs, and just as it was about to sink them into Mark's gut I shouted, *"Stop!"* in the gut worm's language.

Death by gut worm = not a good way to go.

But the gut worm wasn't listening to me. It lunged toward Mark like a bolt of deadly lightning.

Actions, not words, were what I needed.

"Help!" I screamed at the top of my lungs as I leaped from my cot and practically flew over to Mark. I lunged at the gut worm, not caring that it might try to attack me—my only thought was saving my friend.

As I grabbed the worm's thick body between my hands and began to wrestle with it, the gut worm hissed, *"The Hell Hound Curse is coming for him . . . you can't save him!"*

Er, like I take my orders from a gut worm!

"Well, the Hell Hound needs to back off!" I replied sharply, in Gut Worm. *"There's no way I'm gonna let my best friend die!"*

Mark didn't understand any of this, but he looked on in horror as the door flew open and Donny and Red charged in.

Red summoned the gut worm's cage from the other side of the room with her mind. The cage door flew open and Donny helped me wrestle him back inside. The gut worm put up an almighty fight—thrashing and snapping its three sets of jaws in rage. It took me, Donny, and Red to close the cage door.

The gut worm was not happy. *"I'll get him!"* he hissed.

"We need to reinforce this cage," I said to Donny and Red. "The snake is not going to take no for an answer."

"The Hell Hound is not going to take no for an answer," Red said, darkly.

"I don't understand," I shook my head. "Mark was fine yesterday. Why would the curse . . . the gut worm attack now?"

Red shrugged. "I'm telling you, kid—the Hell Hound and the curse are like lightning. You never know when they're going to strike. Until we find a way to lift the curse, Mark isn't safe around any animals, or people. There's danger everywhere."

Well, that's just brilliant. *Danger everywhere.* I might as well just lock Mark in a dark closet and throw away the key.

"I'll drop the gut worm off with a friend of mine while this matter is still unsolved," Donny said matter-of-factly, as if I hadn't just prevented the near murder of my best friend. "Better that we keep him away from Mark at the moment."

I looked over at Mark, who was still sitting up in his cot, the covers rumpled around him in a mess. His face had drained of all color and he looked from me to Donny to Red as if we had each sprouted two extra heads.

"You . . . you can talk to snakes?" Mark whispered to me. "And you—" he turned to Red. "You can move things with your mind?"

Great.

If Mark was ever going to find out about the exact nature of my crazy life, this was not the best way.

"Yeah, I guess I've got some explaining to do," was all I could say to him.

There was a loud knock on the Backstage office door.

We all froze in terror. What was behind the

door? Some terrible creature possessed by the Hell Hound Curse? A psycho ax murderer looking for Mark? A Mongolian death worm just itching to stare into Mark's eyes?

"Sammy, it's me," came a familiar voice from the other side of the door.

I breathed a sigh of relief, "Coming, Mom."

She was standing outside with two school uniforms, our school bags, and two bacon-and-egg rolls. "For you and Mark," she said.

I looked at her blankly.

"You need to go to

school, Sammy," Mom clucked. "And you can't go to school without eating breakfast."

I said thank you and carried the uniforms, bags, and rolls inside. I took a bite of one roll and then the other. "I thought I'd test for poison," I mumbled with my mouth full. "Not taking any chances."

"Great! Now even Mrs. Feral can't be trusted not to kill me," Mark sighed.

He sounded as miserable as a molting mongoose, but at least he was talking. An improvement on yesterday. "Here." I handed Mark one of the rolls. "Just don't choke on it. And be careful the buttons on your school blazer don't fly off and try to kill you when you put it on."

"This isn't funny, Sammy," Mark said. "You should have warned me about all this."

"We'll leave you guys to talk," Donny said, pulling Red out of the room and leaving us alone.

"I'm so sorry," I said, turning to Mark. "I would never have let you come to Banshee if I had thought for one second that—"

"When did it all begin?" Mark asked. "All this weirdness. Has it been going on for as long as I've known you? Your whole life?"

"No!" I said quickly. "It all started in the spring when I discovered that Caliban wasn't just a normal puppy . . ."

Mark listened carefully as I told him about my family being turned into werewolves. We finished our breakfast as I explained how I met Donny and Red, and about what they did, and how we'd made a potion that semi-cured my werewolf relatives.

"I guess that explains why I once saw Natty eating raw fish," Mark said, polishing off his last bit of bacon-and-egg roll. "But what about everything else? How come you can speak to snakes?"

We both changed into our school uniforms as I told him about my strange ability to speak to weird animals. I kept an eye open in case Mark's school shirt tried to strangle him as he put it on.

"What about normal animals?" Mark asked as we walked through the zoo. I couldn't believe how calm he was being. Honestly, I was amazed he wasn't running for the nearest hospital to report me as insane.

"No, I can't speak to them," I told him. "Although right now I wish I could . . ."

As we made our way through the zoo I noticed that all the animals—lions, tigers, pigs, flamingos—were staring at Mark. They were all twitching their noses, sniffing his scent as he walked past. My whole body was stiff, on red alert. I was expecting any one of them to burst out of their enclosure at any moment and go for him.

"So what other weird animals are out there?"

Mark asked, oblivious to all the regular animals staring at him like he was their next meal.

I ushered Mark out of the zoo as quickly as I could before I told him all about yetis and Mongolian death worms, about the wish frog and about trolls.

"You've actually *seen* a troll?" he asked, impressed. "A real-life troll? With your own eyes?"

"Not yet," I said as we walked down the street toward school. "But one has been spotted in the area, and Donny's looking into it."

Mark looked impressed. "Cool."

Seriously, this is why Mark is my best friend. He has a Hell Hound Curse on him and less than an hour ago he was attacked by a three-headed snake, but he still manages to think that troll hunting is cool.

"I'm glad you're speaking again," I told him as we walked past the duck pond. I kept a careful eye on the ducks, thinking they could fly up to

Mark and peck him to death at any moment. "I'm so sorry that I kept all this from you. If I'd told you sooner then maybe I could have saved you from . . . But we'll find a way to lift the curse. I promise."

"It's okay, Sammy," Mark said. "At least I know now. Hey—" he smiled, "—maybe once all this Hell Hound stuff is over, Donny could train me to be a cryptozoologist too."

I smiled. "Maybe."

Right then a huge tractor-trailer truck swerved around a sharp corner, heading straight for us. Moving as fast as a possessed gut worm, I pushed Mark into a nearby bush and readied myself for the blow. I acted on pure impulse.

I didn't want to die. All I was thinking about was saving Mark.

But death wasn't coming for me.

The truck swerved again, this time away from

me. Its tires screeched on the road, leaving black
skid marks on the pavement.

I stood, knees shaking, as the truck drove away.

"He didn't even stop!" Mark gasped. "A hit and
run!"

"The driver probably doesn't know what he's doing," I said in utter shock. "As Red said, the curse is like lightning. Once it's on you, you never know when it's going to strike. The driver must have been possessed."

"By what?" Mark gulped.

"By the Hell Hound Curse," I said, terror coursing through my veins.

8 P.M.

I've spent the day stalking Mark like a shadow. We've been dodging death at every step. Here are a few of the ways I had to save his behind . . .

* This morning, in P.E.——a discus, javelin, and shot-put curved through the air toward Mark. I batted them away with a cricket bat.

* Lunchtime, in the library—a massive book fell off the top shelf toward Mark's head. I pushed him out of the way just in time.

✹ This afternoon, in math—Tommy's compass flew off his desk and shot through the air toward Mark's heart. I swatted it away with my textbook.

Keeping Mark alive has been exhausting! He can't go anywhere without me.

"Seriously, Sammy, you don't need to follow me into the bathroom," Mark said every time that I did.

"You never know when a toilet might explode and drown you in toxic sludge," I pointed out.

Miraculously the day passed and Mark is still alive.

If death's dark claws come for him again tomorrow, then I'll be there to fight them off for another day. This is my fault, after all.

Mark and I walked straight to the zoo after school, my eyes peeled for every car, every dog, every suspicious-looking pigeon that came near us.

We were walking past the lions when I saw Mom coming toward us. "Sammy, Mark," she said, "I have some bad news." I took a deep breath and prepared myself for the worst. I wasn't sure how much more bad news I could take. "There's been an outbreak of the Ebola virus at the medical conference your parents are at, Mark. They're both absolutely fine," she said quickly, "but they're being quarantined. They won't be home for a while so you'll have to stay with us for a bit longer."

Ebola = one of the most deadly diseases known to man.

I'm sure it's not a coincidence that the Ebola virus has turned up a gnat's whisker away from Mark when he has a Hell Hound Curse hanging over him.

"Can we spend the night here again?" I asked Mom. "Beelzebub is still pretty sick and I want to keep an eye on him."

Mom nodded. "You can stay with Donny and Red."

Result!

When Mom had walked away I whispered to Mark, "The zoo is the safest place for you."

"I know. But I can't stay here forever. And there's no way I can stay here once my parents get back. Especially on a school night. I won't need a curse on me—they'll finish me for sure!"

Somehow I doubted that was true. I'm sure Mark's parents would let him share a bed with a tiger if they thought it would protect him from harm.

I wished there was something simple I could do to save him.

And then it struck me.

It was so obvious!

"I'll see you Backstage soon, Mark," I shouted, speeding ahead.

I ran through the zoo as fast as my legs would carry me.

Donny and Red were nose deep in dusty books. The wish frog was asleep in his tank. Nothing new there.

I banged on the glass violently. "Wake up!" He opened a lazy eye and flicked out his mega-long tongue.

"My wish," I demanded, lifting the frog out of the tank and holding him up in front of me. "I need to use it. Now."

"I can hop, you know," the wish frog grunted. "No need to carry me around as if I were some sort of common toad."

"I'm sorry," I muttered feebly, "but I really need that wish you promised me."

The wish frog sat back on his hind legs. "How long have you been thinking about this?"

"About five minutes. It's urgent!" I answered quickly.

"Then, no, I won't be granting any wishes for you today, Sammy," the wish frog replied curtly. He jumped off my hand, soared through the air with his front and back legs spread wide, landed on the floor, and started hopping away from me.

I swooped down, trying to catch him. "Come back here, now!" I demanded. "I need you to help me. I need you to grant my wish. You promised me you'd grant me a wish!"

"You need to think long and hard before you make wishes . . ." He hopped away without looking back.

I chased the wish frog out of the Backstage area and into the main zoo. "Excuse me! Escaped Amazon horned frog coming through!" I warned the zoo visitors who saw us. "These little guys are mega-vicious so keep well away!" People cleared a path as I followed the wish frog all the way back to the Backstage gates.

The wish frog looked up at me with narrowed eyes. "Let me in."

"Only if you grant me a wish." I crossed my arms.

"It doesn't work like that, Sammy," he sighed. "Let me back in and I'll tell you why."

What else could I do? He was my only hope.

I opened the gate and he hopped through. I followed him into the office. Mark was there now, making a start on his homework, and Donny and Red were still reading.

"What are you reading about?" the wish frog asked them.

"The Hell Hound Curse," Red answered.

"Trolls," said Donny at the same time.

I noticed that Donny's eyes were red and he had dark circles beneath them. "You look tired," I said.

"I went out looking for trolls last night," he said absently. "Nowhere to be found. I've had no new reports today. He could be anywhere by now—"

"The Hell Hound has cursed my best friend Mark," I said to the wish frog, interrupting Donny. I didn't want to hear about trolls when Mark had a Hell Hound Curse on him. "You have to help me."

Mark shut his school book and his face broke into a gigantic smile. "You must be the wish frog!"

The wish frog nodded wisely and hopped up on to a bookshelf. "And you must be the reason Sammy wants to use up his one wish. But before

113

I agree to grant his request, might I make one suggestion? Have you tried smearing your friend in garlic?"

Excuse me? Did I just hear correctly?

I wiggled my finger in my ear to clean out any ear wax.

"Garlic?"

Mark scrunched his nose up. "I hate garlic."

"Actually, that's not a bad idea." Donny nodded.

"So this garlic theory . . ." Mark said. "What exactly does it involve?"

Half an hour later we were all standing outside in the Backstage yard with a jar of stinking garlic purée.

We got it by mashing up garlic from the zoo café's kitchen. Everyone knows garlic is famed for warding off vampires. But, according to Red, "It has an effect on most supernatural creatures. That's why

we need to test this outside—
in case we poison the pets
by accident."

Test? Poison?

This did not sound
good.

"The reason garlic is
so effective at warding off
vampires—" Donny started
to explain.

"Hang on," Mark
interrupted. "Are you
saying that vampires are real?"

Red rolled her eyes. "Wow, this kid's even less
with it than Sammy!" Gee, thanks Red.

"The reason . . ." Donny went on, "is that it
contains ancient magical properties that have
worked against evil spirits and demons for
generations. In some parts of the world they even
use garlic to cure snakebites and warts."

This did not sound like a convincing argument to me, even coming from Donny.

Red held up the jar of mashed garlic. "We just need to layer it on to you . . ."

As soon as Red opened the lid of the garlic jar I felt my nose hair burn.

YUCK x 1,000!

I don't think I'll ever eat garlic again after today.

Mark started to gag and retch as they smeared the puree all over him. Red slapped some on to his face and Donny coated his hands thickly. It was gross, gross, *gross*.

Red nodded in satisfaction. "Now, go and feed the gut worm and see if . . ."

She was cut off by the sound of something hurtling through the sky toward us. The sound grew louder as the object came closer.

It was a huge black thing, getting larger and larger as it fell.

It was too big to be a bird, too small to be a plane . . .

Whatever it was, one thing was obvious—it was coming for Mark! The garlic was not working!

"Everyone, take cover!" shouted the wish frog.

He leaped away as Red dived in the opposite direction. Donny and I lunged for Mark at the same time, knocking him off his feet and sending him flying through the air.

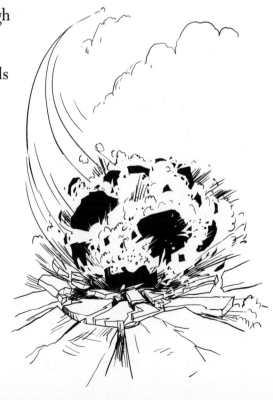

A few seconds later an asteroid about the size of a pumpkin smashed into the earth— landing right where Mark had been standing. It shattered on impact, leaving a small crater in the ground.

"Death by a freak falling asteroid? Well, garlic clearly doesn't work." Red raised an eyebrow.

Watching Mark narrowly escape death by asteroid attack was at least an 8 on the Feral Scale of Weirdness.

Honestly, you could not make this stuff up if you tried.

I looked over at the wish frog and narrowed my eyes, "About that wish . . ."

The wish frog hopped over to me and sighed. "I can grant your wish for you, Sammy, but there's something you need to know about wishes, and curses, and any such thing you will meet and meddle with in your life. Once a curse has been set into motion, there is no destroying it unless you destroy its source. In this case, the Hell Hound. I could grant your wish and save Mark, for now, but the curse would not disappear, it would simply be redirected."

I was confused.

"If the curse cannot have Mark," the wish frog continued, "then it will come for someone else. Most likely someone close to him. Maybe his mother or father, or maybe you."

I gulped. "I don't care, I just have to save—"

"Think about this carefully, Sammy," Donny said. "The wish frog is right."

"I always am," the wish frog agreed with a nod and a heavy blink of his bug-like eyes.

I put my head in my hands in despair. "I have to save him. I'll do anything . . ."

"There is one other thing we could try," Red said.

I looked up hopefully into Red's goth-makeup eyes. "Yes?"

"Phoenix feathers," Red said.

"What an excellent suggestion," grinned the

wish frog. "And to think, Sammy, you might have wasted your wish on—"

"How exactly is a phoenix feather meant to help Mark any more than your stupid garlic did?" I snapped.

"Think about it, Sammy," Donny said, standing up and brushing the yard dirt from his pants. "The first day after he saw the Hell Hound Mark was here—at the zoo—all day, and we didn't have one run-in with death. And he spent that whole day sitting by the phoenix cage covered in feathers."

Mark could be saved by a feather?

Sounds about as likely as a friendly great white shark to me. But we don't have a better idea . . .

Tuesday, September 15

Mark has spent the whole day with a phoenix feather in his blazer pocket and he hasn't taken his blazer off once. And amazingly, he has survived the entire day without biting death dust.

Maybe the feather theory isn't so crazy after all.

After school Mark and I went straight to the zoo. We were heading for Backstage when Grace's boyfriend, Max, one of the zookeepers, caught up with me. "Sammy, Ollie the ostrich has got his beak caught in the sand. I need someone to help me pull him out. Have you got a moment?"

I glanced over at Mark. The feather seemed to be working so I decided a few minutes away from him wouldn't hurt. "I'm gonna help Max out. I'll meet you Backstage."

Mark nodded and walked off. As I turned back to Max something on the ground caught my eye, glistening gold and red in the late-afternoon sunlight.

The phoenix feather.

It had fallen out of Mark's pocket.

Before I could scream after him, a swift movement in the corner of my eye had my head swiveling around.

There was a rogue alligator heading straight for Mark!

Chaos broke loose.

Children were screaming. Adults were running away and taking shelter wherever they could. The zoo visitors parted like the sea in a storm as the alligator charged through.

He moved like a demon possessed—but he had eyes only for Mark.

Mark stood frozen to the spot, too frightened to move as the deadly beast stormed toward him.

I dived for the ground, picked up the feather, and sprinted toward Mark. The alligator was seconds away from my best friend.

"Mark, catch!" I launched the feather into the

air and it flew like a streaming dart of golden light.

Thank goodness Mark is good at catching. He leaped into the air and snatched the feather just as the alligator opened its jaws, inches away from him.

The alligator stopped dead in its tracks. It snapped its mighty jaws shut and looked around in confusion.

Max approached the great beast warily. "Nothing to see here." He waved away the visitors. "Everything is under control." He turned to me. "Sammy, quick, get the alligator leash."

I sprinted to the office, grabbed the leash, and headed back to Max. Together we managed to return the alligator to his enclosure. After that I quickly helped Max get Ollie the ostrich's head out of the sand. Then I joined Mark and the others Backstage.

Mark had already filled Donny, Red, and the wish frog in on the alligator incident.

"So it seems like the feather's working then," Red said smugly. "Told you it would."

I hate it when Red is right.

"But just because Mark is safe doesn't mean the curse has vanished," she continued. "The longer Mark dodges death, the more danger the rest of us are in. The curse will come for someone else if it can't get Mark. It's only a matter of time."

"We've been busy while you were at school today," croaked the wish frog, and I felt a pang of jealousy—I wanted to spend my day Backstage being busy with them, not at school. "We've put together everything we know about curses and how they might be broken."

"Great," Mark said hopefully.

Donny took over. He told us everything they

knew about curses. It took him ages—my stomach was grumbling by the time he'd finished.

Here are the most important facts about curses:

* Curses are as old as time itself. Even the ancient Egyptians were at it—everyone's heard of the Curse of the Mummy's Tomb!
* A curse can grow stronger over time.
* A curse can be passed on to family members or friends.
* A curse is only as powerful as the demon who cast it.
* Destroy the demon, and you break the curse for good.

"Okay, so we need to destroy the Hell Hound," I said. "But we knew that much before. What we really need to know is *how* to destroy it. Any leads?"

"We're still working on it," Donny grumbled.

What a waste of a day!

"What else can we do to keep Mark safe?" I asked, annoyed.

There *had* to be something. Right now, I'd make Mark dance in the rain with frogs if I thought it might help him.

"I suggest we sew the feather into your pocket," Donny said helpfully. "That way there's no risk of you dropping it again. And here . . ." Donny handed Mark a few more feathers. "I took these from my phoenix today. He's still young, so they're a bit fluffy, but they should do the trick."

I glanced at the clock on the wall. "I really need to do my zoo chores before I go home or Mom will kill me."

"I'll help. That way they'll be done quicker," Mark offered.

Hmm, phoenix feather or not . . . I wasn't happy about Mark helping.

"You stay here," I told him. "It's safer."

I went about my zoo chores feeling as if the gray sky was crushing me. How had I let everything go so horribly wrong?

We were no closer to figuring out why the Hell Hound was killing people, or how to destroy it once and for all. And we were no closer to saving Mark from doom.

Just when I thought things couldn't get any worse, my big sister came charging toward me like a steamroller.

"OUT OF MY WAY!" she bellowed.

"Grace, chillax!"

She looked furious. Her face was bright red and she was gritting her teeth and clenching her fists.

"What's wrong?"

"The Biker Boys still haven't responded to their soirée invitation. I've tried calling them, e-mailing them. I even went to their offices and camped out on the sidewalk overnight so I could speak to them. Why won't they reply?" she wailed.

I had nothing to say to her. I wish that the stupid Biker Boys were the worst of my problems. As Grace dramatically stomped off I thought to myself, Things really can't get much worse than this . . . can they?

Wednesday, September 16

What was I thinking?

Things can always, always get worse. And the Feral Scale of Weirdness can always, always crank up, up, up.

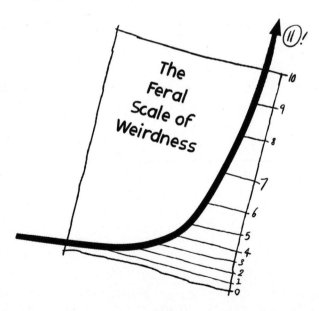

"The troll." Donny was pacing up and down the Backstage office, shaking his head. "He's been spotted again. And he's on the move—any guesses where he's been seen? In exactly the same place as the Hell Hound. This is more than just a coincidence. Is the troll following the Hell Hound? Why? I need to find out! I'm going out every night looking for it. I haven't slept for days. When I'm not troll hunting I'm researching bridges and trolls and—"

"Er, excuse me," I interrupted, letting my school bag fall to the ground. "Never mind the troll. What about the Hell Hound? What if it strikes again? What about Mark?"

"Yeah, what about me?" Mark asked.

"We're drowning here, Sammy," Donny said. "We've got too much on our plate. I just can't shake this suspicion that the troll and the Hell Hound are somehow connected." I stared at him blankly. "Okay, so we need a plan," I said firmly.

Red crossed her arms. "We're listening . . ."

I straightened my shoulders and gave everyone jobs, just as I'd seen Donny do a million times . . .

Donny—keep looking for the troll.

Red—keep researching the Hell Hound.

Me and Mark—keep Mark alive!

"Can't I help Donny with the troll?" Mark asked.

Was Mark as crazy as an aardvark flying an airplane? "No, Mark, *way* too dangerous. You're staying right where I can see you."

Honestly, a troll could knock on my window and try to eat me for dinner and I still wouldn't care. Unless it knows how to destroy the Hell Hound, I just don't want to know.

Trolls = *Not. My. Problem!*

When I got home my mood was fouler than fox poop.

Mark is spending the night on a cot in my room with a phoenix feather under his pillow. Maybe this way his pillow won't suddenly try to swallow him whole or something equally deadly.

"Sammy," Mark whispered as we lay in the darkness, "I had no idea your life was so crazy. And now mine is too."

"I'm sorry," was all I could think to say.

"I'm sure we'll be able to fix this Death Curse thingamajig," Mark said. He sounded a lot brighter than I felt. "I mean, you've dealt with loads of life-and-death-type situations before. Werewolves,

super-freaks, Mongolian death worms . . . You've always been okay."

It feels good that Mark has so much faith in me. I just hope I don't prove him wrong. I hope that I can find some way to keep him alive.

Friday, September 18

The worst sound in the world (apart from the Biker
Boys' new album) is the sound of Grace screaming.

At dinner this evening Grace shoved this letter
in my face:

Dear Grace Feral,

We are delighted to accept
your invitation to attend
the Feral Zoo Soirée. We
would also be honored to
perform some of our smash-
hit songs for your guests.

Yours sincerely,

The Biker Boys

"We'll set up a stage by the parrot cages," Grace said, talking at 100 miles an hour. "And they can do their dance routines against a backdrop of colorful parakeets . . ."

"This is delicious, Mrs. Feral," Mark said, shoveling food into his mouth. Mom had cooked sausages and mashed potatoes. Mark and I had our sausages cooked with gravy, and everyone else just ate theirs raw.

"Thank you, Mark," Mom replied, smiling. "I must admit, I wasn't very happy with Sammy when he told me you knew about our . . . situation. But it's so nice that we can all sit and have dinner together. It's great that we don't have to hide who we really are from you."

"We used to be werewolves." Natty nodded wisely, sneaking some of her sausage to Caliban, who was sitting by her feet.

"Hey, it's almost like I fit in around here, now I have a Death Curse." Mark grinned.

Everyone stopped eating and stared at Mark in horror.

I hadn't told anyone in my family about the Hell Hound Curse—obviously! "Ha ha ha! Good one, Mark," I laughed. "That's really funny!"

He looked at me, confused.

"Shut up!" I whispered.

"Why?" he mouthed at me.

I rolled my eyes. "Trust me." Mom would FLIP like a pancake if she knew.

"Maybe we should put together our own guest list for the party, Sammy," Mark said quickly, changing the subject. "Like zoology professors and nature documentary makers. People who could help the zoo."

"That's a really good idea," Dad agreed.

So Mark and I spent the rest of the evening drawing up our own invite list.

It's been so nice hanging out with Mark since he's got his phoenix feather that I almost forgot all about the Hell Hound Curse. For a few hours this evening I almost believed we were normal again.

And then I got this text from Donny:

Come 2 the zoo 2morrow. I'm taking a day's break from troll hunting. Let's get this Hell Hound on a leash once & for all.

Who am I kidding? I'll never be normal. I'm Sammy Feral—weirdo supreme. I live my life by the Feral Scale of Weirdness. Why should I spend my Saturday doing anything other than trying to destroy a Hell Hound Curse . . . ?

Saturday, September 19

Two heads are better than one. And five heads (Donny's, Red's, mine, Mark's, and the wish frog's) = the Research Team Supreme!

We have had a day smashing through Donny's crypto-books like never before. Donny and the wish frog have been reading the ones in weird languages, Mark and I have been reading through everything in English, and Red has been on the Internet.

We worked for hours and hours in silence, and every now and again someone would look up and share an interesting fact that they had learned about the Hell Hound, a clue that might help us break its power and lift the curse once and for all.

It was my job to write everything down (I do like writing, after all). I could even write another chapter of my guide to the Hell Hound if I wanted to . . .

Sammy Feral's Guide to the Hell Hound

Chapter 2

* Other names for the Hell Hound include: the Black Shuck, Dip, Gytrash, and Warg (Warg is my favorite).

* No one has ever, ever escaped the Hell Hound Curse.

* The Hell Hound is a solitary creature and operates alone.

* It HATES water and is never spotted by streams, rivers, ponds, or the ocean.

* The Hell Hound cannot move on from a place until its curse has claimed a victim.

"If the Hell Hound is a solitary creature," Mark pondered aloud, "then I bet it hasn't been hanging out with the troll. Maybe there isn't a link between them at all—it really is just a coincidence that they've been visiting the same places."

"Hmm, or maybe the link we're looking for isn't between the Hell Hound and the troll," Red suggested. "Maybe it's between the places."

Donny pointed at Red's computer and said, "Quick, print a map of the area. I think I have an idea."

A few minutes later Donny had stuck the map to the wall. He took a marker pen and drew a circle around all the towns that Miss Oxley reported the Hell Hound had visited: Devilbottom, Wraith, Shadowston, and Banshee.

As soon as he'd circled the places the pattern was obvious. But he drew a line between each town on the map, connecting the dots so it was clear to see.

"It's moving in a straight line," Red whispered. "And it's coming straight for us."

Yep.

Next stop on the Hell Hound trail of destruction = my town. Tyler's Rest.

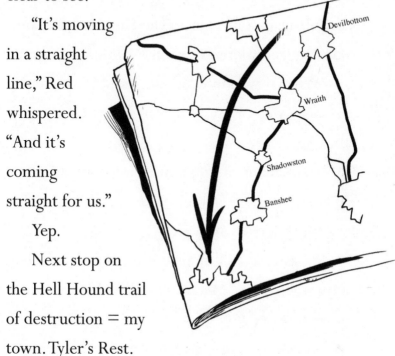

"Okay," Donny said, breaking the silence. "This is good. At least we now know there's a pattern."

"A pattern that's heading straight for us!" the wish frog gulped.

Mark laughed nervously. "It could still just be a coincidence."

Donny shook his head. "Like I said, I've been a cryptozoologist long enough to know there's no such thing as coincidence. The Hell Hound is on a warpath, and we're in its way."

"Why?" I wondered aloud. "And if it's coming through Tyler's Rest, then why haven't we seen it already?"

"Remember, it can't move on until its latest curse has worked," Donny said.

We all looked at Mark.

"So as long as I'm alive, then the Hell Hound stays where it is," Mark said. "Unless it appears to someone else first . . ."

"Let's focus on trying to destroy this thing," I said, trying to lighten the mood. "If the Hell Hound hates water so much, then that must be some kind of clue."

"You think we need to find a way to drench it?" Mark said. "Lure it into a river somehow?"

"Worth a shot," I grinned. "And as long as Mark

is alive, the Hell Hound is trapped in Banshee. So at least we know where to find it."

Today was a good day. I feel like we're finally getting somewhere.

Now all we have to do is come up with an awesome plan to lure the Hell Hound into water . . . how hard can it be?

Sunday, September 20

Mark and I came to the zoo first thing today for another round of Hell Hound brain-storming.

We found Red in the Backstage kitchen making pancakes, and Donny fast asleep on the sofa.

"Hey, Donny, wake—"

"Shh," Red warned me. "He's been out all night in Banshee looking for the troll. He's only just gone to sleep."

That did not make me happy!

I leaned over Donny and gave him a short, sharp shove.

"Troll!" Donny's eyes flew open and he sat up in alarm. "Is it here?"

"No, the troll's not here, Donny," I said, annoyed. "We're here—me and Mark. And we need to do more Hell Hound planning. We had such a good day yesterday. You promised you'd put troll hunting on the back burner until we had this stuff figured out."

"Sorry," Donny yawned. "But I had another

e-mail last night after you guys had left. Someone saw the troll under a railway bridge, but when I arrived there was no sign. I'm so close to catching him, I just know it. Oh, and, Sammy—" he looked up at me with sleepy eyes "—I forgot to tell you yesterday that I've heard from Genghis. He's coming to stay!"

"Who's Genghis?" Mark asked.

"A Mongolian death worm—a friend of ours," I answered absently. Mark stared at me as though I'd just offered him a plate of yogurt-coated wasps for dinner. "When's he arriving?" I asked Donny.

"Any day," Donny answered. "He's just stopping in for a night to say hello. He's heading up to visit his cousins in the Outer Hebrides. Lucky really—he might be able to shed some light on the Hell Hound Curse . . ."

"Er, am I the only one who's a bit freaked out by the thought of a death worm?" Mark gulped.

"I mean, I've never met one before, but the name doesn't exactly make me think that they're cuddly creatures."

"Like Sammy said," Red grunted. "Genghis is a friend."

Genghis *is* a friend. And Donny's right—maybe he can help us out. If anyone knows about creatures that kill you with a look, then it's Genghis.

Come to think of it, I should probably get some sunglasses for Genghis to wear around Mark, just in case . . .

Friday, September 25

I know, I know—four days is a long time not to write in my diary. But I've been super-busy and just haven't had the time. I'd be here all day if I wrote down every little detail of the last week—so I'll make this as snappy as a cranky crocodile . . .

This last week we have:

* sent out party invitations to every zoologist in the country
* helped hundreds of zoo visitors to have their photo taken with Humphrey the hawk

* had no more run-ins with death, thanks to Mark's trusty phoenix feather
* sent a message to every resident in Banshee warning them about a dangerous ghostly dog on the loose (no more Hell Hound sightings so far—result!)
* prepared everything Backstage for Genghis's arrival
* worked on a totally awesome plan to DESTROY the Hell Hound once and for all!
* wasted far too much time at school. Why they make me go there is a complete mystery.

We don't want to risk putting our plan into motion until Genghis arrives. Why? Hmm, it's complicated—I'll explain once he gets here.

But so far he's yet to show his wormy face at the

zoo. I've even picked him up a cool pair of shades so he can shield his death stare. I'm itching for him to arrive. I'll be as happy as a sea lion with his head in a bucket of fish when he does!

I am ready to bring this Hell Hound DOWN!

Saturday, September 26

"I've had some excellent news," Dad announced at breakfast this morning. "Every single zoologist we've invited to our soirée has agreed to come!"

Party! It's a *party*!

"That's awesome, Dad," I said.

If every zoologist in the country is coming to our party, then we have a great chance of getting them to help us raise money for the zoo.

"And what about all the TV stars and famous people?" Natty asked, chomping on a strip of raw bacon before feeding the fatty bits to Caliban. "Famous people are more important than zoo people."

Before I could argue I felt my phone buzz in my pocket.

It was a text from Donny.

> Genghis has arrived! Time 2 test-run that plan of yours!

"Gotta go," I said, stuffing the last of my toast into my mouth.

"Don't forget your zoo chores, Sammy," Mom said impatiently.

"I'll do them this afternoon—I promise—but this morning I said I'd help Donny out with something. Mark, you're coming too." I hoped that Mom wouldn't press me for details. I don't like telling her about all the stuff I get up to with Donny. She'd freak out if she knew that (once again) I'd gotten myself into a deadly situation.

Why do Moms always worry so much?

Mark and I hotfooted it to the zoo. I was *so* excited to see Genghis!

GENGHIS
* **Species:** Mongolian death worm.
* **Looks like:** Giant worm with HUGE fangs.
* **Powers:** Spits acid and can kill you with a single look.
* **Friends with:** The wish frog, the yetis, and just about every other strange creature out there.

Genghis is mega-grouchy, but he's not a bad guy. And I know he'll want to help out when he hears that Mark's in trouble.

You see, the thing is, Genghis is the closest creature I know to a Hell Hound. He's not a ghost, but he could kill me with a single look. I can't think of anyone else that would make a better Hell Hound stand-in. This is why we've been holding off on our Hell Hound–drenching plan.

We need to practice on Genghis. I'm sure he won't mind.

I mean, how angry can a little bit of water make a Mongolian death worm?

Surely not angry enough to spit at me . . . to stare at me . . . to kill me . . .

As the Backstage gate swung open, Mark and I were greeted by the sight of Genghis the death worm with the wish frog perched on the top of his head.

"Mark, look at the wish frog and not Genghis," I warned him. Mark scrunched his eyes shut tight, just to be sure. *"Genghis! It's good to see you!"* I said in Death Worm. *"I've bought you these to wear."* I handed him the sunglasses.

"Let's speak in English, Sammy," he said. A great big globule of deadly acidic spit flew in my direction, and I leaped aside to dodge it. "I haven't spoken it in a while and I need to practice. Sunglasses are a good idea—we should have thought of that before."

"You're just in time for breakfast, Sammy," the wish frog croaked as I balanced the glasses on Genghis's wormy head. "Pancakes sound okay?"

Pancakes sound great!

Technically I'd already eaten breakfast . . . but that wasn't going to stop me. So we joined Donny, Red, and Mark in the Backstage offices and we all dug into pancakes with maple syrup.

"It's great to see you again, Genghis," Donny smiled. He looked mega-tired. He must have been out troll hunting again last night.

"I came as soon as I heard," Genghis said seriously. Although, at that moment, taking Genghis seriously was as tough as a tortoise's shell. A giant worm wearing sunglasses was a total 10 on the Feral Scale of Weirdness.

"Heard what?" I asked.

"That the zoo is in danger," he replied.

"Er, hang on," I said with a mouth full of pancake. "What are you talking about?"

"Word on the crypto-street is that there's a dark force heading for Feral Zoo," Genghis said. "Something ancient and powerful has the zoo in its sights, and it wants to destroy it."

"The Hell Hound!" Donny, Red, Mark, and I all said at once.

"What does the Hell Hound have against Feral Zoo?" I said in panic.

"I don't know," Genghis replied, spraying the table with acidic spit. We all jumped back. "Sorry," he apologized. "All I know about the Hell Hound is that the earliest sightings were on the other side of the world. But over the centuries it has been getting closer. It seems as if it's following a path heading straight for the zoo. As soon as it has claimed a victim, then it moves on to its next stop. It never goes back."

I wrinkled my eyebrows in confusion. "But it's stuck in Banshee as long as Mark is alive. And as long as it's there it's powerless. It can't strike in the same place twice."

"Of course it's not powerless—the opposite in fact," he replied. "The longer a person lives after the curse has been put upon them, the stronger the curse will become, and the more vengeful the Hell Hound will be. The more vengeful it is, the more likely it will strike again in that very same place—it won't stop until someone has died, it won't let anything get in its way. What possible grudge could a Hell Hound have against a zoo?"

"What about trolls?" Donny asked. "What do you know about them?"

Genghis shrugged his wrinkly body. "About as much as I want to know. They're one of the most ancient of crypto-creatures—nearly as old as dragons."

Red shook her head angrily. "Never mind the troll, we need to focus on the Hell Hound—it's heading our way. Time to snuff out that pesky pooch once and for all."

I felt a sharp pain in my leg. Mark was kicking me under the table. I looked over at him and he mouthed the word "water" at me.

I nodded my head. There was no time to lose. The Hell Hound had to be stopped and we had an idea that might just do that. It was time to put my cunning plan into action . . .

"After breakfast, Genghis," I said, trying to sound casual, "we should take a walk around the zoo. We've had some work done since you were last here—they've re-fenced the vulture cages and—"

"Aren't you worried about the zoo visitors seeing me?" Genghis said.

"The zoo isn't open for another hour or so," Donny said. He knew how important the plan was, and we had to test-run it on Genghis! "Leave the Hell Hound worrying to us. You should go with Sammy."

After our delicious second breakfast, Mark and I led Genghis out into the main zoo, leaving the others Backstage.

"You've definitely got your phoenix feather?" I asked Mark.

He rolled his eyes at me. "As if I'd go anywhere without it."

I tried to focus on putting the plan into action and not on the CRAZY fact that Genghis had just told us—that the Hell Hound had it in for the zoo.

Mark and Genghis got to know each other as we walked through the zoo. I kept reminding Mark not to look him in the eye—Genghis might be wearing shades, but I didn't want to risk it.

As Mark kept Genghis distracted with facts about wasps, I led us past the zebras, large cats, and other African animals, and around the birds of prey and the penguin enclosure. Eventually we walked out onto the large lawn in the middle of the zoo—where zoo visitors can have picnics in the summer. When we were right in the middle of it, I signaled to Donny and Red. I knew they were watching and waiting nearby.

All of a sudden, the sprinkler system whirred to life. Water burst out of the ground around us like upside-down rain.

We were SOAKED!

"Argh!" cried Genghis. *"Are you trying to drown me?"* he shouted in Death Worm.

162

"We're going to lead the Hell Hound into a sprinkler system and drench it," Mark said, looking pleased with himself. "We thought we'd practice on you."

Genghis let out an angry hiss and spit flew on to the ground, making the lawn under our feet sizzle.

"Well, I'm pleased I can be of assistance to you,"

he said through gritted fangs. "You could have told me this was what you were up to!"

"I wanted to see how difficult it would be to lure a creature to water without being able to look at it," I confessed.

"You intend to get so close to the Hell Hound that you can lead it toward a sprinkler system?" Genghis said.

I nodded.

Genghis exhaled loudly. "Sammy, it won't work. You can't defeat the Hell Hound. It's impossible."

"There's no such thing as impossible," I told him.

And I believe it.

The practice run is complete.

Tomorrow it's time for the real thing. I'm going back to Banshee. I'm going to walk around the graveyard until I know the Hell Hound is watching me. Then I'm going to lure it toward the house that Miss Oxley is staying at. The house with the sprinkler system in the garden. And then I'm going to drench it.

I'm going to break that curse once and for all!

Sunday, September 27

I went about my zoo chores this morning with a soupy feeling in my stomach. I was nervous and excited all at once. Part of me couldn't wait to go back to Banshee and lead the Hell Hound to its death, but part of me was terrified.

After I'd finished restringing the monkey climbing nets I went Backstage.

"I'll be gone by the time you come back," Genghis said as he wriggled up to me. "I have family expecting me in the Outer Hebrides tomorrow—it's quite a journey so I need to make a move."

"It was great seeing you," I said. "And I'm sorry about the whole water-soaking thing."

"I usually like some warning before I am attacked by water," he grumbled. "But I'm pleased I came. At least someone's warned you that the Hell Hound has its sights on Feral Zoo. And, Sammy . . ." he paused—I wished I could look him in the eye and guess what he was thinking—". . . good luck. You're going to need it."

After a lunch of sandwiches from the zoo café, Donny, Red, and I got ready to leave. "You're staying here," I told Mark. "No arguments."

He looked at me impatiently. "I'm already cursed, Sammy. What more can the Hell Hound do to me?"

"You need to leave this to the professionals, kid," Red said, slinging a backpack over her shoulder.

Me? A professional? Wowzer!

"Do me a favor and stay by the phone?" Donny asked Mark. "If more troll sightings come in, I want to hear about them as soon as I get back."

"I'll see you later this evening, Mark," I said, trying to sound kind. I always hate it when I'm left out of an adventure—even a dangerous one. "Keep an eye on everything for us while we're gone." Mark straightened his shoulders and nodded with pride. "And don't lose your phoenix feather!" I warned.

Donny, Red, and I drove to the village of Banshee in silence. I ran through the plan again and again in my head. All I had to do was lead the Hell Hound into the sprinkler system and give Donny and Red the signal to turn the water on.

The closer we got to Banshee, the more I thought about the plan. And the more I thought about the plan, the more I realized just how stupid it was. So many things could go wrong. What if the Hell Hound didn't show up? What if I looked it in the eye before I had a chance to drench it? What if the sprinkler system was broken? What if something happened to Mark while we were gone?

After the long drive Donny pulled the van up by the village graveyard. It was getting dark outside.

There was no more time to worry about everything that could go wrong. It was time to rock 'n' roll.

"We'll meet you at the house, like we planned. We'll be ready for you," Donny said seriously. "You've got a phoenix feather, just in case?"

I nodded and patted my trouser pocket. "Make sure you're well hidden," I warned Donny. "I'll shout when I'm there—no hand signals this time. I don't want you guys to risk a glance toward me . . . toward the Hell Hound."

Red's eyebrows crinkled in thought and she said quietly. "Good luck, kid. You're brave."

Wow, Red thinks I'm brave.

I guess I am. Brave or stupid.

Donny and Red left me alone at the gate of the graveyard.

I walked in slowly.

The sound of the wind rushing through the trees made the hairs on the back of my neck stand at attention. I shivered as I stepped further into the dark graveyard. I made sure to keep my eyes on the ground. I didn't once look around at the crooked gravestones that poked through the earth.

I walked around the graveyard, circling the church at the center of it. After one circuit there was nothing to tell me that the Hell Hound was near. I kept on walking, around and around, weaving in and out of the gravestones as though they were some kind of maze.

I don't know how much time passed. An hour, maybe two. The air got colder and the night got blacker.

I was freezing. I was starting to think that this was a waste of time. Maybe Genghis was wrong and the Hell Hound's Curse wasn't growing stronger just because Mark was still alive. It wasn't about to strike again. The Hell Hound wasn't going to come for me.

But then I smelled it.

A dank, horrible stench crept up my nostrils and ice began to flow through my veins. My heart skipped and then beat furiously in my chest.

It was near. And it was coming for me.

Very, very slowly, I turned around and began to walk. I closed my eyes and opened them the tiniest of peeps so I could only just see the ground in front of me.

I walked back toward the graveyard gate.

The smell followed me as I walked. It was working. The hound was following me.

My heart was beating so fast I thought my

chest was going to explode like a combusting phoenix. I'd never been this close to death before, not really. It felt horrible. I could smell it in the air and feel it creeping all around me.

Careful not to look up, and not to open my eyes any wider, I left the graveyard.

The smell stayed with me. My plan was still working. The Hell Hound was right behind me.

Slowly I led the ghostly shadow away from the graveyard, down the road and to the big house where Donny and Red were waiting for me as planned.

The smell was getting stronger as I walked toward the house. I knew that at any moment the hound would find a way to appear before me—it would find some way to make me look up and into its eyes. Then I'd be history. My fingers twitched nervously toward my trouser pocket and touched the phoenix feather that was poking out at it. Yep, it was still there.

There were just a few more steps to go . . .

I quickened my pace toward the front lawn and I felt it follow me. As soon as my feet touched down on the grass I broke into a run.

"NOW!" I screamed at the top of my lungs.

The sprinkler system pumped into action and water cascaded around me, drenching every bit of me. I kept on running, but Red's voice made me spin around. "Sammy, your feather!"

I whirled around to see the feather flying out of my pocket and falling to the ground, heavy with drops of water.

I reached down to pick it up, and that's when I saw it.

The horrible, ghostly dog was standing right before me and staring straight at me. Its teeth were as sharp as vampire fangs, its eyes red hot as flames. Water whooshed through the air but the Hell Hound didn't care.

The water wasn't doing anything to stop it. It wasn't killing the Hell Hound, it wasn't breaking the curse. Rivers of water cascaded off the Hell Hound's back and it didn't even care.

The plan had failed.

I had failed.

And I was staring straight into the eyes of the Hell Hound.

I knew with absolute certainty that I was next.

It had cursed me. And I was going to die.

Wednesday, September 30

Somehow I have survived three days without dying.

"The curse will be magnified now that there are two of you under it," Donny said surprisingly calmly, once we were back at the zoo that night. "Phoenix feathers will hold it off for now, but we still need to find a way to crush it for good. And if one of you . . . or both of you—or someone close to you—dies, then the Hell Hound will come after the zoo. I just wish we knew why. Maybe then we'd have a better idea of how to stop it."

"Water was a dumb idea," I pointed out. "Next

time I have an idea like that please put a smelly sock in my mouth."

I have glued phoenix feathers to the inside of my school blazer, to the soles of my shoes and to my pillowcase. I have even taped them to my body like armor. Thankfully the phoenix's feathers grow back almost instantly—otherwise he'd be as bald as a plucked chicken by now.

But I can't spend the rest of my life covered in phoenix feathers. If I don't bite death dust soon then someone will, and I can't let that happen. I have to find a way to stop the curse for good.

Maybe this is it for me. Maybe I was never meant to grow up and be a cryptozoologist.

But every time I look at my family, every time I listen to Natty whine about sausages, or Caliban yap, or Grace sing along to the Biker Boys, I feel so sad.

I don't want to die.

I can't die.

I won't.

But if I don't die then the curse might come after my family. I could never live with myself if something happened to them.

There must be something I can do.

Thursday, October 1

With our phoenix feathers as protection, Mark and I have been getting as cocky as cawing cockerels these last few days.

Er, brain-flash, Sammy—WHAT WERE YOU THINKING?

I could have a whole flock's worth of phoenix feathers taped to my body, but the curse would still be on me . . . and what's worse, it's getting stronger.

Mark's parents got the all-clear of the Ebola virus and today Mark's going back to live at home. After school I walked him to his house.

"I'm starving," he announced, as we walked down the street. "All this death-dodging really works up an appetite. I hope Mom and Dad have stocked the fridge since they got back."

Mark has his own house key but he didn't need it. Both of his parents were already home.

"Come in, son," his dad said sadly, opening the front door. He grabbed Mark and pulled him into a smothering hug. Er, embarrassing! He squeezed him so tightly I thought Mark's eyes were going to pop out. He squeezed and he squeezed, and he wouldn't let him go. Was something wrong? I was just about to start wrestling Mark's dad when he let go and said, "It's so good to see you, Mark. But I have some terrible news."

"What's wrong?" Mark said nervously. "Where's Mom? Is she mad because she found out I'd been staying at the zoo?"

Mark's dad fell silent.

Something was DEFINITELY wrong.

Usually Mark's dad can't wait to say something mean about the zoo—about fatal animal diseases, parasites, and dangerous claws, jaws, and animal stings.

"What's happened?" I asked Mark's dad quietly, dreading the answer.

Before Mark's dad could reply, a horrible wailing sound blared out of the living room.

"Mom?" Mark's voice trembled.

"Mittens . . . !" she wailed.

Huh?

"Mittens?" Mark said in panic, speeding toward the living room. "What's wrong with . . . ?"

As we burst into the living room I nearly leaped out of my skin at what I saw.

Mark's family cat was frozen, in the middle of the room. His back was arched, his teeth bared, his eyes nearly popping from his head. His fur stood on end and his tail was raised and ready to whip into attack. It was if he'd been turned into a statue.

"Mittens is dead!" Mark's mom wailed as she sat sobbing in a nearby armchair.

I've spent my life hanging around a zoo, and I'm sad to say I've seen a few dead animals in my time. But none of them have ever, ever looked like that.

"When did this happen?" I whispered.

"We came home earlier today and Mittens was fine—Mrs. Robins next door did a splendid job of looking after her while we were away. But then I popped out to the store to buy some milk and I came back—" Mark's mom sniffed, "—and found Mittens like this. No pulse, no sign of injury. It's as if she's been . . ."

"Scared to death," I finished for her.

"How could this have happened?" Mark's dad shook his head sadly.

Mark and I exchanged a look of horror, and he said exactly what I was thinking. "We need to get to the zoo."

"Now the curse has taken its next life, the Hell Hound will be coming straight for the zoo," I announced.

We were all gathered in the Backstage offices. The wish frog narrowed his eyes in thought. "This can't be the work of the Hell Hound. The Hell Hound can't leave Banshee."

Donny was pacing up and down and Red was nervously twiddling the skull necklace around her neck.

"He's right. This could be something else entirely. Maybe I should go out to your house, Mark," Donny suggested as he prowled. "Examine Mittens's body for signs of—"

"NO!" Mark and I both shouted at once.

Mark's parents had had enough to deal with for one day. A gray-haired teenager spinning tales of a Hell Hound Curse could only make things worse.

"We know what we saw," I told everyone. "It's definitely the work of the Hell Hound."

The wish frog was sitting on a nearby bookshelf. He leaped on to my shoulder and whispered in my ear in Wish Frog, so only I could understand, *"If things get much worse then you won't have a choice but to use that wish of yours. Whatever the consequences."*

I shuddered. *"But won't others die if I use my wish?"*

"It looks as though that's already happening," he replied.

"Both Sammy and Mark are cursed at the moment," Donny said, pausing and looking at the magical frog on my shoulder. "Maybe that has somehow given the Hell Hound enough power to leave Banshee. And now that it's cursed Mittens, and Mittens has died, there'll be no stopping it. We need to protect the zoo."

"How do we know it's coming after the zoo?" Mark asked. "Genghis could have been wrong about that."

"Don't be stupid, kid," Red groaned. "Any rumor that you hear on the crypto-scene is usually true."

I hated to agree with Red, but she's right.

"We need to protect the zoo," I said quickly. "Tape phoenix feathers to every animal enclosure, sew them into the clothes of everyone who works here, put them in the hands of everyone who passes through the gate."

"Sammy's right," Donny said gravely. "But that's

not all. If the zoo really is the Hell Hound's final target, then it'll be looking for a way to strike big, take as many lives as possible."

"When would it have the opportunity to claim hundreds of lives?" Red pulled her painted eyebrows together.

The answer struck me like a slap from a dead fish.

"The zoo party," I said with horror.

Silence flooded the room and everyone's face drained of color. Even the wish frog turned a sickly shade of green.

"What are we going to

do?" Mark's voice was shaking like a rattlesnake's tail.

"We armor up with phoenix feathers," Donny said, so quietly it was menacing. "And we let it come to us . . ."

"Let it come to us?" Mark shouted. "Why would we do—"

"We lure it into a trap," Donny cut him off.

"But what do we do once we have it trapped here?" I asked. "Remember how our last trap turned out."

"We stop it, once and for all," Donny said with no trace of humor.

I stared at him blankly. "How?"

He closed his eyes. "I'm not sure yet, but we have nine days to come up with a plan so deadly it can destroy a Hell Hound Curse."

Friday, October 2
7 days until the zoo party . . .

Operation Hell Hound Curse is officially ON!

So far, so good. There have been no further sightings of the beastly dog and no new deaths.

And it's time to pop open the cola and dance the samba, because I have a clue that will help me muzzle that devilish pup once and for all.

Well . . . I think I do . . .

Today our schoolteachers let us put up Halloween decorations. It's not till the end of the month, but I reckon the teachers use it as a bit of an excuse not to teach us for a couple of hours. Every kid in school was busy drawing giant spiders to tape up in the hallways, spraying fake cobwebs around the lights, and carving pumpkins.

Mrs. Palmer cornered me in the lunch room as I was digging into a slice of pizza. "Sammy, I know how much you like writing . . ." My heart sank. Was she going to get me to do something mega-boring like write an article for the school newspaper? ". . . And we'd like to ask a few students to come up with fun Halloween names for the lunch menus over the next couple of weeks. Would you like to have a go? You won't have to go to math this afternoon—you can sit in the library with the other students and work on your ideas."

I don't need to be asked twice to skip a math class.

"Of course, Mrs. Palmer." I smiled.

There were four of us in the library trying to come up with spooky food names this afternoon.

A girl in the year above me who stank so strongly of perfume I thought she'd damage my sense of smell, and two boys from the older years. I'm not sure how old they were, but their skin was very pimply.

We spent about ten minutes coming up with ideas. Here are a few of my favorites:

* Wriggling Worms with Zombie Brains (spaghetti Bolognese)
* Vampire's Delight (tomato soup)
* Fallen Angel Spew (jelly and ice cream).

But soon the conversation turned serious, and everyone started talking about Halloween and spooky things like ghosts. I kept mega-quiet as I didn't want to give anything away about the Hell Hound. The perfume-stinking girl was blabbing on about the time she thought she'd seen a ghost. "It was at my grandma's house," she said excitedly. "I got up in the middle of the night to go to the toilet and there was the ghost of an old lady standing at the top of the stairs."

"Are you sure it wasn't your grandma?" one of the older boys snickered.

"Positive," the girl said with certainty.

Then she said something that made my ears prick up and got me thinking . . . "Ghosts are spirits with unfinished business. I've always wondered what the old lady's was . . ."

Never mind the old lady in stink-girl's grandma's house! I knew a ghost far deadlier— and maybe the Hell Hound had unfinished business with the zoo.

I texted Donny as soon as I got out of school:

Ghosts R spirits with unfinished business. We need 2 find out what the Hell Hound's is. Maybe then we can stop it.

Donny texted back right away.

Out on troll patrol. Come
by the zoo 2moz. U might
be on 2 something.

Hurry up tomorrow and bring on the crushing of
the Hell Hound Curse!

Monday, October 5
4 days until the zoo party . . .

The last few days have been a whirl of getting ready for the zoo party, all while keeping a beady eye out for the Hell Hound.

The countdown to the zoo party is *on* and we still don't know how we're going to defeat the Hell Hound. Yesterday Donny rounded everyone up and gave us all jobs to do:

Me—Discover the Hell Hound's unfinished business

Mark—Put up phoenix feather defenses around the zoo

Red—Research, research, research

Wish Frog—Prepare to grant that emergency wish, if all else fails

Phoenix—Keep on giving feathers

"What about you?" Mark asked Donny curiously.

"Donny's got other things on his mind at the moment," Red said bluntly.

"Nothing that's more important than crushing the Hell Hound Curse, surely?" I asked.

"It's these troll sightings." Donny pushed his gray hair aside with a restless sigh.

"I've never not been able to find a creature before."

Honestly, these bogus troll reports are getting on my nerves.

"Are trolls even dangerous?" I asked.

Donny frowned. "Sometimes . . ."

"Well, the Hell Hound is dangerous all the time," I said, annoyed. "So I think the Death Curse that's looming over us all is a bit more important than some grumpy troll."

Red rolled her eyes. "The troll might be useful to us, Sammy."

Er, unlikely . . .

"I've told you before—I don't think it's a coincidence that the troll keeps appearing. I think it has something to do with the Hell Hound. And trolls are very wise," Donny said thoughtfully. "If there's any creature that might know how to defeat a Hell Hound . . ."

"It's a troll?" I finished.

So let me get this right . . . the only creature that could possibly help us is not only a troll, but a troll that doesn't want to be found. Fantastic. NOT!

Tuesday, October 6
3 days until the zoo party . . .

The wish frog was waiting for me at the school gates this afternoon.

"You know you're not meant to leave the zoo," I reminded him. "You're the last of your kind. You're too important to be squished by a car, or eaten by a cat . . ."

"But I have this," the wish frog lifted his front leg and pointed at the phoenix feather taped haphazardly around his head. He looked like some kind of Cherokee frog chief.

I rolled my eyes. "So is this just a social visit, or was there something you wanted to see me about?"

I walked down the street and the frog hopped by my side. He leaped on to a nearby car. "Let me sit on your shoulder so we can walk and talk."

He hopped up there. "I walk, you talk," I said. "What's up?"

"You need to come to the zoo . . . now . . ."

"But I'm on my way home," I told him. "I have a ton of homework to get through and I still need to discover what the Hell Hound's unfinished business is."

"That will have to wait. They've found the troll . . ."

W.H.A.T.??

"Er, were they going to tell me?" I asked, feeling annoyed. I hate it when Donny and Red leave me out of their investigations.

"They figured you have enough to worry about at the moment without—"

"I'm going straight there."

Donny and Red were huddled around the Backstage computer when I burst into the office, the wish frog still on my shoulder.

"And when were you going to tell me that you've found the troll?" I almost shouted, slightly out of breath from running so fast. "Have you spoken to it yet? Does it know how to break the curse?"

Donny scratched his gray head of hair. "We haven't spoken to it. And, Wish Frog—do you have to tell Sammy everything?"

I glared at Donny. "You're forgetting one very

important detail: I'm the only one who can speak Troll. If you want to talk to the troll about the Hell Hound, then you need me with you."

Red crossed her arms. "You know I hate to admit it when the kid is right, but . . ."

Donny sighed and nodded his head. "There's something you should see . . ."

He spun the computer screen around to show me a grainy black-and-white photo. In it I could make out what looked like a hunched, wart-ridden giant, crouching under a railway bridge. "Is that the troll?" I asked.

Red nodded. "And we think we know where that bridge is. It's just a few towns away."

"Are we going there this evening?"

"Yes, but the wish frog stays here," Donny said seriously. "Trolls have been known to eat anything in their path. I can't risk the wish frog's life."

But we can risk *our* lives, I thought.

"We leave after sunset. I'll pick you up from home. Tell your parents we're going looking for bats or something and that you'll be staying with us afterward. Have a good dinner and dress warmly."

I nodded, taking mental notes of Donny's instructions.

"And, Sammy," he added, "do as much research as you can into trolls before I pick you up. You need to know what we'll be facing."

"I told you," the wish frog croaked. "No time for homework tonight."

No time for homework *ever*!

I have spent the last couple of hours looking on the Internet for facts about trolls.

This is what I have discovered:

TROLLS

* **Looks like:** Crooked and knobby with bulging eyes and a very large nose.
* **Diet:** Bones—human, animal, or anything else they find.
* **Can be found:** Under bridges.
* **Interesting fact:** Can only be seen if they want to be.

"Sammy! Donny's downstairs and ready to take you bat-hunting," Mom's just shouted up the stairs at me.

Gotta go . . . will report back as soon as I can . . .

Wednesday, October 7
2 days until the zoo party . . .

Last night . . .

. . . I was way too tired to write in my diary. We didn't get back to the zoo until after sunrise this morning. Good thing I'd told Mom I was going bat hunting and then staying at the zoo or she'd have given me a total blasting for staying out all night and getting no sleep.

But there was no time for sleep.

Not when I had a troll to interrogate.

Donny and Red picked me up shortly after sunset and we drove to the village where they thought the troll was currently living.

"The thing about trolls, Sammy," Donny told me as we drove, "is that they only appear to you if they want to be seen."

"I know—I figured that one out last night. Is that why you haven't seen it before?"

He nodded his head. "I suspect so. For some reason it's shown itself to other people, but not to me."

"So, trolls can turn themselves invisible?" I tried to work out how on earth that could be possible. I mean, I'll believe almost anything these days, but invisibility? I don't think so . . .

"Not exactly," Red told me. "Trolls are cunning tricksters, and they have ways to avoid being seen if they don't want to be."

Well, that makes about as much sense as a chocolate lion cage on a sunny day.

"So what makes you so sure we'll see the troll tonight?" I asked.

205

Donny shrugged. "I'm not sure of anything at all . . ."

He parked by an old railway bridge that crossed a river, and we got out of the van. It was now pitch black outside and freezing cold. Thankfully I had worn my yak-wool sweater and thermal pants for the occasion.

We walked under the bridge. Rusty tin cans, potato-chip bags, and bits of trash were strewn all over the riverbank. There was a shopping cart in the river, and an old shoe floating alongside it. Gross.

I crinkled my nose. "The troll could have chosen a nicer place to live."

"Trolls love grime and garbage." Red's lip curled in disgust. "This is a perfect troll habitat."

I should have known then that any creature who chooses to live somewhere so revolting was bad news . . .

We had a quick search under the bridge, but there was no sign of the troll. "What now?" I asked Donny.

His words came out accompanied by warm puffs of air. "Now we wait."

So we waited. We waited for hours and hours in the freezing cold, the three of us huddled against the wall of the rusty bridge. The sloshing of the river and the hooting of night owls were the only sounds that broke the silence—no troll footsteps, not even a troll hiccup or sneeze.

"We should go back," Red said grumpily after we'd been there for what felt like decades. "He's not coming out tonight."

I cast her an angry glare. We couldn't just go back—that would be giving up. I hate giving up.

I had to do something drastic to get this troll to show itself to us . . .

"Listen, troll!" I shouted. "We've come to find you because we need your help. We know you're here. We know you're listening. My best friend and I have the Hell Hound Curse on us. And not only that—the Hell Hound is on its way to Feral Zoo. And if you don't help us, then soon every animal and person there will be dead!

If you know anything about the Hell Hound Curse, anything at all that can help, please show yourself to us . . ."

As the last echo of my voice bounced off the railway-bridge beams, I hung my head in despair. It hadn't worked. The troll wasn't coming out.

"Please," I begged, one last time. "Tell us . . . we can offer you anything you want in return . . ."

"Fee, fi, fo, fum . . ." came a grumble from the shadows. The voice was speaking a language I'd never heard before, but I understood it right away. He was speaking Troll. *"I smell your blood and bones, you better RUN!"*

"It's here . . ." I whispered, the breath catching in my throat.

Donny leaped forward, excitement etched on his face. "What did it say?"

The troll spoke again. *"I like the taste of little boy's bones . . . yum, yum . . ."*

"You really don't want to know," I said. *"Please,"* I begged the troll. *"We need your help."*

There was a horrible noise—a bit like a snarl—and then the troll said, *"And what makes you think I want to help you?"*

At that moment the creature appeared right in front of us.

It wasn't tall—about my height—and its bulbous nose was touching the tip of mine.

I screamed and jumped back so quickly I fell on my butt. The troll loomed over me with a half-smile on its ugly mouth. Lank hair hung around its wart-covered face.

Donny and Red gawked in silent astonishment—I guess it wasn't just me who had never seen one of these up close before.

I scrambled up off the ground and tried to stand up to the troll and look brave. *"Do you know the Hell Hound?"* I asked.

The troll cackled like a wicked witch. *"The cursed beast that haunts the night. The dark one who walks the line between the living and the dead."*

"So you do? You know him?" I asked with hope.

"I know all of the things that lurk in the shadows. All creatures of the night that feast on humans. The Hell Hound takes your soul . . . I only take your bones . . . yum, bones . . ." He licked his warty lips. *"But don't worry . . . I only take the bad children, the rotten ones, the ones who don't behave."*

I gulped as I quickly explained to Donny and

Red what the troll was saying. I also made a mental note to NEVER misbehave again—no way do I want my bones to become troll food!

"Ask him what he can tell us about the Hell Hound. How can we break its curse?" Donny said. I quickly repeated the question in Troll.

"What will you give me if I tell you?" The troll leaned toward us, his eyes narrow with menace. *"You cannot have something for nothing. There must always be a price."*

"What do you want?" I asked.

The troll tilted his head back and regarded us thoughtfully before he spoke again. *"I have a story for you, boy. I am old. Very, very old. Older than you, or your parents. Older than your town and older than the languages you speak. For centuries I have roamed the Earth, but I haven't always been alone. I had a family once. A beautiful troll wife and two small troll children. The Hell Hound took them from me. One*

212

night, when I was off hunting for naughty children to munch for dinner, the Hell Hound appeared before my family. They died the next day. I have been alone ever since. I HATE the Hell Hound for taking them away from me. And I have sworn to destroy him, no matter what it takes. For years he has evaded me. I never knew where he would strike next . . . and then I learned of a place where I would be certain to find him. A place that he is traveling to, where he has unfinished business . . ."

"Feral Zoo." I shuddered. "But why? What did the zoo ever do to the Hell Hound?"

"He wasn't always a beast of the night. He was once a normal, happy dog. His mother was the beloved pet of one of the zookeepers. She had puppies and they were happy. But the keeper sold one puppy to a brute of a man who mistreated him. The cruel man didn't feed the dog; he left him outside in the rain and punished him frequently.

But a dog can never hate his master, no matter how cruel that master might be. Instead, the dog focused all his hateful energy on the zoo— the place that gave him up. He swore that after he died he would get his revenge.

He's spent his ghostly days working his way back there, destroying everyone in his path—including my family. I will tell you how to defeat him, but I ask for one thing in return . . . that you let me help you bring him down."

Maybe I should have taken a moment to think. I was agreeing to work with a creature that ate human children. Maybe I should have stuffed a sock in my mouth and stayed quiet.

But I didn't.

"I promise you," I said, without a pause. *"You have our word that we will defeat the Hell Hound together."*

I quickly explained to Donny and Red what the troll was saying.

"This is bad news." Donny shook his head. "Sammy, trolls are liars and tricksters—we don't even know if he's telling the truth!"

"We don't have a choice but to trust him," I said. "The zoo and everyone in it is in danger—we can't take any chances."

Red rolled her eyes. "He hasn't even told us how we can defeat the Hell Hound!"

"How can we defeat him?" I shouted at the troll, shaking like a leaf on a windy day.

The troll cackled a horrible laugh that made my bones rattle in terror. *"There is only one way,"* his voice boomed beneath the bridge, "to defeat the beast of the night. It is the way of Narcissus."

Narci . . . what?

"Narcissus?" I managed to repeat. "Narcissus?" I said again in English.

Both Donny and Red looked at me in confusion.

"The myth as old as the gods of Olympus," the troll continued. "That is the only way you will defeat the beast."

"What's he saying?" Donny pulled at my sweater.

"Something about the gods of Olympus," I told him, confused.

"The ancient Greeks?" Donny muttered.

"Now you will know how you can defeat him . . ." the troll said. As he spoke he started to drift in and out of visibility. Like a flickering candle flame before it goes out. "I will be there to help you when the time comes. You have my word . . ."

And then the troll vanished into thin air.

"Don't go . . ." I shouted. "That's not enough for us

to go on. How will you help us when the time comes? I don't understand!"

But the troll had disappeared completely.

We stood there for ages, shouting and hoping the troll would come back, but he never did.

The sun was coming up, and morning mist was rising off the stinking river.

I feel SO angry. The troll didn't tell us anything we needed to know. We know nothing! If the Hell Hound's unfinished business wants to destroy everything at the zoo, then we're as stuffed as a chipmunk's cheeks at harvest time.

And Narcissus? The gods of Olympus? I have no idea what the troll meant by all of that.

"Narcissus . . . Narcissus . . . Narcissus . . ." Donny kept repeating on the way home.

"What do you think he means?" Red asked, looking exhausted. The black bags under her eyes were as heavy as a raccoon's.

"I'm not sure yet," Donny muttered. "I'm not sure."

Who or what is Narcissus?

And what does it have to do with the Hell Hound?

Thursday, October 8
1 day until the zoo party . . .

Maybe having to go to school isn't such a bad thing after all.

No, I'm not as crazy as a kickboxing kangaroo.

School came in pretty useful today. The school library, to be precise.

Why?

Narcissus, that's why.

I went to the library at lunchtime to get on the Internet. But there wasn't a computer free so I had to do some research the old-fashioned way.

"Why do you want a book of Greek myths?" The

librarian eyed me suspiciously. She's used to me asking for books on tropical frogs and poisonous snakes, not ancient legends. "What do you want to know, Sammy?"

I figured I might as well tell the truth. "I want to know about Narcissus."

She nodded and led me through the library to a shelf that was labeled MYTHS AND LEGENDS. She ran her finger over the books until she found what she was looking for, pulled it out, and handed it to me.

Ancient Greek Myths.

"You'll find what you're looking for in there," she said.

I took the book to a nearby table and read for the rest of my lunch hour. I found out all about Narcissus, and what I found out was very, very interesting indeed.

Check this out . . .

NARCISSUS

* Narcissus was a good-looking and very proud hunter in ancient Greece.

* He was totally OBSESSED with himself—mega-arrogant, in fact.

* He loved to stare at his own reflection in mirrors, glass, and water.

* He was tricked into staring at his reflection in a pond for so long that he died.

There's an obvious link between Narcissus and the Hell Hound . . . only it wasn't obvious to me right away. In fact, at first I was completely baffled by the story. I had no idea what it had to do with the Hell Hound or curses or me and Mark.

I should have been paying attention in French this afternoon, but instead I spent the class whispering to Mark. I quickly filled him in on everything that had happened with the troll and what I'd discovered about Narcissus.

"What do you think it means?" I asked him.

"Total mind-blank, Sammy," was all Mark could say. "I have no idea what that means. Although this Narcissus guy sounds pretty vain!"

After school I went to the zoo and headed Backstage.

Luckily for me, the wish frog was the first thing I saw.

He listened to my story carefully and then said almost right away, "Well, you know what the obvious link is, don't you, Sammy?"

"They both think way too much of themselves?"

The wish frog shook his head. "Water," he said simply. "Water."

OF COURSE!

The answer was staring me in the face as clearly as Narcissus's reflection in that pond.

Yes, the Hell Hound is afraid of water. But it's not being drenched that it's scared of, like we thought. It's afraid of its own reflection . . . and if it's afraid of water, then I bet it's afraid of mirrors too.

"Donny! Red!" I shrieked, calling everyone into the Backstage office. "Get everyone else— the zookeepers and Mark. I'll get my family. Meet me back here in an hour. I have a battle plan!"

I sped around the zoo like a galloping gazelle, rounding up my family. I found Dad in his office, Mom cleaning out the warthogs' enclosure, Grace showing a line of children how to hold Humphrey the hawk, and Natty sneakily eating raw fish out of the penguin-feed bucket.

"Why are we all Backstage, Sammy?" Mom said, sounding annoyed. "What is all this about?"

"Tomorrow is the party," Dad reminded me, as if I'd forgotten. "I've got rather a lot to do between now and then. I don't have much time—"

"This is important," I interrupted, as Donny and Red joined us. I took a deep breath, "Okay, everyone. I need to tell you something. But you've got to promise not to freak out, because everything is going to be okay. I have a plan. But you should all know that there's a Hell Hound Curse on me and it's coming for you too. And tomorrow night we might all die."

Wow, that got their attention.

Silence burned my ears as everyone's jaw fell open.

So I told them the whole story as they stood

there stunned and silent. I told them about the Hell Hound and that it had cursed Mark and now me. I told them it had come to our town and killed Mark's cat, and that it wanted to destroy everything at the zoo (I left out the part about the troll—they had enough to worry about for one day). And then I told them all about my plan.

Donny was the first person to break the silence. "It's a good plan, Sammy."

"I don't know." Dad shook his head, looking as pale as a polar bear. "We're risking everyone's lives—every zoologist in the country will be here tomorrow night. We're using them as bait!"

"And the Biker Boys!" Grace gasped.

"What if we can't stop this hound thing . . . ?
What if it gets them too . . . ?"

Trust Grace to worry about that!

"It won't," I reassured her. "Not if I have anything
to do with it. This plan has to work. Everyone
knows what they have to do tomorrow, right?"

Everyone nodded and there were murmurs of
agreement.

I smiled a smile of victory. "Then that's final.
Tomorrow we destroy this thing once and for all."

Friday, October 9
The day of the zoo party . . .

The night of the zoo party began smoothly.

I stood with my family at the entrance to the zoo, greeting people as they arrived.

As Mom and Dad shook hands and welcomed TV personalities, zoologists, and reporters, Grace, Natty, and I gave everyone a phoenix feather.

"Won't everyone think we're cruel?" Natty asked. "They'll think we stole the feathers from the birds."

"There are no real birds in the world that have feathers like this," Grace pointed out—

holding up a shimmering gold phoenix feather. "People will think they're fake."

Grace was right.

"Are these for some kind of raffle?" asked one lady zoologist as we gave her a feather.

"Yes," I said quickly. "There are dozens of amazing prizes to be won. But to be in with a chance you must keep this feather on you at *all* times."

As more and more people filed into the zoo, Grace started to chew her nails, twirl her hair around her fingers, and hop from one foot to the next with excitement, "Why aren't they here yet?" she whined.

I was just as anxious as Grace. Don't get me wrong—I think the Biker Boys are the worst thing to happen to mankind not counting the Hell Hound Curse—but if I wanted my plan to work then I needed them to show up.

Eventually we heard the faint roar of

motorbikes in the distance. Grace squealed like a piglet as the headlights of five bikes blinded us. As the bikes screeched to a halt at the Feral Zoo gates, five teenage boys climbed off and grinned. "We're the Biker Boys," one of them said, crossing his arms. "And we're here to rock your night into the stratosphere . . ."

I'm not sure what's worse—death by Hell Hound Curse or spending the night with the Biker Boys.

But I had to be nice to the cheesy boy band. I needed them on our side if my plan was ever going to work. "Welcome to Feral Zoo." I smiled at them. "My sisters will show you where the stage is and help you get ready."

Grace and Natty scuttled off toward the parrot enclosures with the Biker Boys, leaving me with Mom and Dad.

Soon all the party guests had arrived, and I ran to find Donny.

He was with Red, Mark, and the wish frog, huddled near the ocelot enclosure.

"Okay, Donny—you go and wait for the troll," I instructed. "As soon as he arrives, tell him what we need him to do. Red, you go and tell the Biker Boys that we need their help."

"Why do I need to be the one to speak to the

Biker Boys?" Red complained. "Just listening to their so-called music gives me a rash. The sight of them might make my eyeballs explode. Can't Grace do it?"

"I can't trust Grace to be around the Biker Boys without melting into a puddle of gushing girliness. You have to be the one to do it, Red." She rolled her eyes and snorted in disgust. "Mark," I continued, "make sure the wish frog is out of harm's way, and then help me round people up . . ."

"I don't see why I can't be of more help," complained the wish frog.

"You know why," I said with a sigh. "You're the last of your kind. We need to protect you. And besides, we don't want anyone to know we have a wish frog here. It needs to stay a secret."

"Okay," he reluctantly agreed. "I'll be in my tank if anyone needs me."

The next hour was uneventful. Guests stuffed themselves with party food, chatted, and laughed. The zookeepers gave guided tours of Feral Zoo, telling everyone about our special breeding programs, our extra-large enclosures, and how we've won "Zoo of the Year" three times. One of the zookeepers had organized an auction, where guests could bid for a signed football shirt, a lifetime's zoo membership, and bang-up meal for two in the zoo café. There were donation boxes scattered around the place, and I beamed as party guests emptied their bulging wallets into them. As far as fundraising went, the night was looking to be a success. If only the zoo's money problems were all I had to worry about . . .

Then I caught the first whiff of Hell Hound. It was gone as quickly as it came, carried away on the wind, but it was enough to tell me that he was close—he was coming for us.

Soon after that it was time for the Biker Boys to perform.

Mark and I helped round the party guests up so they stood in front of the stage. As everyone huddled together, the smell got stronger. I wondered if the Hell Hound would suddenly appear right then on the stage, in front of everyone. That would not have been good—that was not part of the plan. But as the seconds turned to minutes there was no Hell Hound in sight.

The Biker Boys rode onto the stage looking paler than before (I knew that meant Red had spoken to them—which was good). They launched into their first ear-insulting song of the evening, singing into hand-held microphones and dancing around their motorbikes.

They really were as terrible as a porcupine pillow.

Halfway through their third painful song, the air at the back of the stage began to shimmer.

"Fee, fi, fo, fum . . ." boomed an invisible voice. *"I smell bones . . . yum, yum, yum!"*

People looked around in confusion—this didn't sound like part of one of the Biker Boys' songs. And then, out of nowhere, appeared the knobby, ugly troll.

The air erupted with the sound of screams and shattering glass, as people dropped their drinks.

The troll gave me a mischievous wink as Mark and I went into crowd-control mode.

"Everyone, please follow us to safety!" Together we rounded

the panicked guests up like sheep and herded them toward the lawn in the center of the zoo—the very place where I had lured the Mongolian death worm.

Red had cut the lights, and it was pitch black. My family, Mark, Donny, and Red ushered people back and spread them out. "Keep quiet and stand in the shadows, so the troll can't see you," we whispered.

I was left standing in the middle of the dark lawn.

That's when the smell got stronger and I knew the Hell Hound was close to appearing.

I stood shivering, standing, and waiting.

The smell crept up my nose. It was so strong it made my eyes water.

I had hoped that this many people would be too much for the Hell Hound to resist.

We had lured him to us.

And now he was mine . . .

As the smell became stronger a mist began to form in front of me. And from that mist stepped the terrible Hell Hound. His claws sharp, his eyes like red traffic lights, his breath the stench of death.

I took a step closer to the stinking, deathly beast. We were moments away from springing my plan into action. But I wanted the Hell Hound to explain himself. I looked him square in the eye as I spoke, *"Why?"* I asked him. *"Why take revenge on the zoo? It wasn't the zoo that mistreated you—it was your cruel master."*

"Why?" The Hell Hound repeated the question, narrowing his fiery eyes. *"Do you have any idea what a miserable life I had? A life that could have been so different if I had only stayed here. My master was cruel, but so was the zoo for giving me up. I hate it, and I hate everyone here. You pretend to care about animals, but you don't. I'm going to destroy you all."*

"*No!*" I shouted at him. "*That's not true. People love animals. I love animals—even the ones that might kill me. I know everything there is to know about cone snails and the blue-ringed octopus. I've looked after my pet python, Beelzebub, as if he was a member of my family. And he's mega-dangerous—he even tried to eat my sister once. I'm friends with all animals—even a Mongolian death worm!*"

"*But you're a freak, Sammy,*" the Hell Hound growled. "*Not everyone wants to cuddle a python.*"

I stood my ground and shouted at the beast, "*Other people might be afraid of dangerous animals, but that doesn't mean they want to harm them.*"

"*You sound very sure of that,*" the Hell Hound snarled. "*But I'm not here to listen to you beg. It's too late for you.*"

It's too late for *you*, I thought!

The Hell Hound was beyond saving. He was so lost in his anger and bitterness . . . he'd taken too many lives to ever come back from his dark, dark place. There was no saving him, even if I wanted to.

It was time to crush his hellish power once and for all.

"You're right," I gulped, my feet inching backward. *"It is too late . . ."*

Suddenly the zoo lawn was illuminated by floodlights. Bright white light shone on the terrified faces of every party guest around us.

The Hell Hound was surrounded.

His eyes lit up like flames and he purred in delight at the number of people who were here. Huge globules of thick, smelly drool dribbled from his mouth as he panted in excitement. *"You're all doomed,"* he growled.

Terrified whimpers erupted through the crowd of zoo guests as they felt the Hell Hound Curse fall upon them.

My breath caught in my chest as I wondered if my plan was ever going to work.

Soon the whimpers were drowned out by the rev of motorbike engines. "Coming through!" shouted the Biker Boys in unison. The crowds of party guests parted as the bikes drove up, headlights shining on to the beast.

Their tires skidded on the zoo lawn as they spun their bikes around.

Before the Hell Hound knew what had happened, the band members had angled their bike mirrors so they were pointed right at the hound. He was surrounded by his own reflection.

Bingo!

There was a sudden explosion of light, as if bolts of lightning were striking out from the mirrors toward the Hell Hound. The bike mirrors cracked and shattered on the ground.

"What are you . . . ?" the Hell Hound snarled. *"You tricked me . . ."* He screamed as though his soul was being torn in two. *"You've cursed me! You've cursed me with the strength of every life I've ever taken . . ."* The mist surrounding him turned a violent shade of red and flickered like flames as the Hell Hound lifted his head to the night sky and howled in terror as he began to fade. Like a fire slowly dying out, he burned away to nothing.

And as he puffed out of existence, all that was left was a faint cloud of black smoke and the lingering stench of garbage.

Instantly it felt as though a great weight had been lifted from my shoulders.

"The curse!" Mark shouted, running toward me and smiling. "It's gone—I can feel it!"

"Me too." I smiled back. "It's worked."

I felt the eyes of every party guest on me. Everyone gawked in stunned silence as they tried to make sense of what they had just seen.

"Ta-da!" I shouted proudly. "I hope you all enjoyed tonight's entertainment. Only the best for the Feral Zoo Soirée!"

Ear-shattering silence.

No round of applause. No cheering.

Everyone was STUNNED!

I felt a hand clap me on the back, and I turned around to see Mom and Dad standing behind me. "We're so proud of you, Sammy," Mom said with a tear in her eye. "Once again you've saved the day."

"I couldn't have done it alone," I whispered.

At that moment, soft murmurs broke out

throughout the crowd. Gasps of astonishment, laughter, and wild clapping filled the air as people congratulated us on what they thought was the best show they'd ever seen.

"This zoo needs your help," I said loudly. "Feral Zoo is a very, very special place. We can't let it close down—it must be saved!"

"Please, everyone," Donny said loudly, joining me in the center of the lawn, "tell your friends and colleagues about the work we do, so we can continue to protect the world's creatures."

Applause erupted around me. Shouting, cheering, clapping, and whoo-whooping!

I'm happy to report that there were no more near-death experiences all night. In fact, the rest of the party was a roaring success! Everyone was just so happy to be there and couldn't stop congratulating us on the "amazing puppets" we used in our show.

Zoologists, TV stars, the Biker Boys, and zookeepers joined my family and friends as we danced the night away in celebration. Even the zoo animals seemed to be having a good time. Khan the Sumatran tiger, Humphrey the hawk, and Charles Darwin the chimp all looked on as we partied.

"You can keep the feathers," I told everyone, when the time came for them to go home. "They'll bring you luck."

"We'll donate all the profits from our new single to the zoo," one of the Biker Boys said as their motorbikes rolled out of the gates. "And we'll come back and do a show here whenever you want."

"Thank you." I made a mental note to buy some earplugs in case they did ever come back.

The zoo had emptied of happy party guests when a familiar crooked and wart-covered troll waddled up to me.

"Are you going back to your bridge?" I asked the troll.

"It's my home. Where else would I go?" it grumbled back.

"You could stay here, if you promise me you won't eat any more children," I said. *"Not even the bad ones . . ."*

The troll frowned at me, considering my offer, *"That's a lot to ask, Sammy. But seeing as you have just defeated the Hell Hound, I'll think about it . . ."*

Well, I guess that's better than nothing.

Soon the zoo was empty, and somehow I found myself alone by the parrot cages with just the sound of the zoo's nocturnal animals for company. The Hell Hound *and* a troll at Feral Zoo—tonight really maxed out the Feral Scale of Weirdness.

Man, I love this place. I might have nearly died here more times than I can remember, but I'd do anything to save it from closure—even listen to the Biker Boys.

I guess today was a great success. We raised money *and* defeated the Hell Hound and lifted the Death Curse.

Wow, I'm getting really good at this cryptozoology thing!

Saturday, October 10

Dear_____

Thank you for attending the Feral
Zoo Fundraising Soirée!

Thanks to your generous contribu-
tions, we have raised more than
enough money to save the zoo
from closure.

We are delighted to offer you and
your family lifelong membership
of Feral Zoo, in thanks for your
generosity.

Yours sincerely,
The Feral Family

I wanted to add a bit to the letter about enjoying the phoenix-feather souvenirs, but Dad decided that we didn't need to remind people of anything strange that had happened here.

Mom and Dad sat me down this morning and gave me a very stern talking-to about getting myself into dangerous situations. "You could have been killed, Sammy. What were you thinking, going off in search of the Hell Hound in the first place?"

"It's my job," I argued back. "I'm a cryptozoologist, just like Donny and Red. I have to go after weird creatures like the Hell Hound, and the troll, no matter how dangerous and deadly they are. Besides—" I sighed, "—everything turned out all right in the end, didn't it? And now we've defeated the Hell Hound, Miss Oxley is going to reward us with £1 million, and I'm donating my cut to the zoo. We'll—"

"Never have to worry about money again," Dad finished.

Mom is still annoyed that I went chasing after the Hell Hound at all, but she'll come around. "From now on I want to know everything you're getting up to, Sammy," she said. "Even when it's dangerous."

"Sure, Mom," I agreed reluctantly, crossing my fingers behind my back.

I know enough about cryptozoology to realize that I'll be getting myself into a few more life-and-death-type scrapes in the future . . . Let's hope Mom doesn't mind the next time I have to go off in search of a fire-breathing newt or a two-tongued dragon!

Sunday, October 11

FERAL ZOO TO OPEN NEW WING!

The world-famous Feral Zoo has announced plans to open a new research laboratory for rare and dangerous animals. Its construction and running costs have been funded by generous donations and it is due to open next year.

The new wing will provide rehabilitation and breeding programs, as well as state-of-the-art terrain to mimic natural habitats. A new on-site laboratory will also open, to conduct research into anti-venoms.

The paper also said that the zoo will appoint a specialist zoologist to run the new wing. Three guesses who that will be . . . Donny!

Yep, Donny and Red are staying at Feral Zoo

and will be in charge of running the new crypto-center. In fact, they used their share of Miss Oxley's reward money to pay for it.

I'm as happy as a snake on a sunny day.

But there's something *even* cooler than that to report. Guess who's going to be Donny's new laboratory assistant . . . ME! "No one knows as much about crypto-anti-venoms as you do, Sammy," Donny told me. "After all, you were the one who discovered the werewolf cure."

Donny's even agreed to let Mark come help out from time to time. Awesome!

I have to stay in school (no getting out of that one) and Mom says I still need to do my regular zoo chores. But I'm totally psyched that I'll be spending so much time Backstage as a professional cryptozoologist.

Oh, gotta go . . . another cryptozoology request has just come in . . .

Apparently there have been sightings of a mermaid in the Thames.

"Mermaids have the worst sense of direction," Red grumbled as we packed a bag and prepared to drive into London to check out the report.

"I know," agreed Donny. "If I had a penny for every mermaid we've had to give directions to . . . I'd be able to build *two* new wings at Feral Zoo!"

Life is as weird as a fish climbing a tree. But I love it, and I wouldn't change a thing.

I'm off to meet a mermaid . . . Over and out.

ACKNOWLEDGMENTS

Once again, thank you to everyone who's helped make this book possible. Thank you to Sarah Lambert, Alice Hill, Niamh Mulvey, Talya Baker, and everyone else at Quercus Children's Books, and to Sam Brown and John McColgan for supporting me on my first ever author tour! Thanks to John Kelly for his spot-on illustrations, Victoria Birkett for her enduring support and advice, and to Luke and the rest of the Hawken/Willis clan.

And thank YOU for following Sammy's weird adventures!

ELEANOR HAWKEN is the author of many books for children. She created and wrote the Will Solvit adventure series under the pseudonym Zed Storm, and also writes ghost stories for older readers. Eleanor works in publishing in London and was a founding member of the Bath Festival of Children's Literature.

JOHN KELLY is a prolific children's book illustrator and author, as well as a digital concept artist for the film industry. Among his many books are *Guess Who's Coming to Dinner* and *Scoop!* Kelly lives in London.

Find out

how Sammy discovered his cryptozoology
skills in the first book in this awesome series!

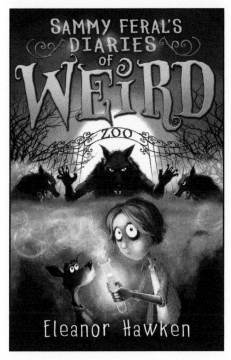

Out now!

Watch out!

The Feral Scale of Weirdness is about to hit an all-time high!

A Mongolian death worm needs Sammy's help!
His best friend, Bert the Yeti Chief, has gone missing.

Can Sammy summon the Ministry of Yetis and rescue Bert?
He's going to need help from his old friends Donny and
Red, not to mention a very reluctant wish frog . . .

Out now!